SUSURRUS *ON* MARS

ALSO BY **HAL DUNCAN**

from LETHE PRESS:

Scruffians!: Stories of Better Sodomites

Rhapsody: Notes on Strange Fictions

*

THE BOOK OF ALL HOURS:

Vellum

Ink

Testament

The Boy Who Loved Death

Errata

An A-Z of the Fantastic City

Escape From Hell!

Songs for the Devil and Death

SUSURRUS ON MARS

HAL DUNCAN

LETHE PRESS

Published 2017 by Lethe Press

ISBN: 978-1-59021-683-5

Cover and interior design
by INKSPIRAL DESIGN

I

•

Barefoot, trimmed in pirate slops of: white linen britches to his knees; doublet unbuttoned to air his carnelian chest; red Monmouth cap of Phrygians, French or Phobian revolutionaries. Master Jaq of the Flaxblond Scruff, Esquire, scrambles a rope ladder of hemp and hardwood, brigantine rigging between an English Oak and Silver Linden grown from grafts of Robin Hood's own secret GHQ and the very tree Carl's father Nils sucked his teeth at as he frowned out over his Swedish homestead, searching for a family name to replace the patronymic *Ingemarsson* on his admission to the University of Lund, settling on the lind tree, settling on *von Linné,* which his son Carl would AKA to *Linnæus*. And now here they are, far elsewhen and elsewhere, oak and linden, two tree trunk masts grown centuries into each other's canopies.

Satchel slung over his shoulder jouncing, Jaq scrambles up through thickening leaf scent and rustle to a crow's nest cabin treehouse, ramshackle perch looking south, past a prow jut of basalt fo'c'sle, over a meadow of perennial ryegrass, leftover of ley farming, over his sward Sargasso rolling down to shores of copse, far hedgerowed fields and hills beyond his acre, the woods and glints of the Rio Erehwyreve beyonder, and beyonder even, the snowy peak of Euripus Mons, ten miles to the south.

The sky is blue and broad as the summer's span unfolding before him.

Latitude minus forty five degrees of arc, longitude one hundred four, Jaq sites himself by the sun and the fob, golden shirt-stud and silver scythe in the sky respectively, the latter a shattered scattered moon, it tickles him to know, Phobos of his forefathers. Two hundred miles inland east of the Hellas. Two twenty seven pee em on Saturday, first of Resh, six seventeen New Common Era. Sails set out of five sharpish months of spring, months short in stint, skin-tight in span, but ever so keen in shift. Sails set out of certainty.

•

PUK'S VOICE, FROM inside:

Thirty one days in Alef, Daleth, Zayin, Yod and Mem.
Thirty one days in Ayin too and Qof and Tav, and then?
All of the rest have thirty days, but one year every five
There's three more days for us all to play
Cause the leapfest has arrived.

A wean's rhyme made for the questioning years afore enabling that Jaq can scarce imagine now let alone mind, whole other eon of infancy poldered by touchscreens and tutor interfaces, not just *knowing* that the Martian year has twenty-two months, fourteen of thirty days and eight of thirty-one, evenly waltz-stepped but for the bookend finish and start months nestling side by side in the clasp of the cycle, six hundred and sixty eight days in total each year, with a three day leapfest every fifth year, which Jaq discovered was fun for a three year old, all parades and pageantry weaving through the Old Town at the height of summer, straining to see the peacock-pinioned hussars on their quaggas till his Papa hoiked him to his shoulders—discovered was even more fun for an eight year old in the evenfall stretching to midnight bonfires on the braes out of town, getting moroculous on home-made poitín, mangled on mushrooms with Joi, Shim and Don, high wasters of adolescent abandon draped in glass beads won by feats of audaciously sordid stancing, Shim flashing tits, Jaq fluffing tarse, and more, lying on their backs in the grass after it all, scented with each other's sweat, looking up at the stars and the fob, the luster of necklace worn by Mars himself sparkling in the indigo for eyes widened by psilocybin.

His PAN not long enabled, he ran his fingertips through the grass and babbled the wonders gushing up from the hylenet, theories of hunter-gatherer evolution sparked by entheogenic use as rendered in the mesolithic rock art of the Tassili n'Ajjer, rituals in Mesoamerica and recreation in pre-Interregnum Xanthe, the chemical structure of 4-hydroxyl-methyltryptamine, the looping and lolloping of sense rendering the shift of time as palpable as it could ever be to the human mind, the span of it too, mass being energy coiled, energy being time—extent, action and potential rearticulable as axes of six dimensional timespace, events as topologies, every force a form, every form a force.

He can scarce clench in his nous now how it was before, let alone savvy how Puk must feel, newly-enabled to hylenet access and extra-shook surely, raised with the whole interworld an infernal Sodom decried by his Geister kith—barring the geisted parents and sis Ana who brought her sixer bro here for the sanity. The rhyme, Jaq tracks, sprung from a call via his matelot's PAN, natürlich, the immigrant simply savouring access to a childhood he never had on Earth where everyone is always already twice as old as they are really.

Wild to think.

Jaq unslings the satchel from his shoulder as his barefeet slap planks warmed by the sun, the treehouse true Tarzanian, upturned claws of oak and linden branches cradling a rough hut with railed Widow's Walk all round, achieved by: the pack will of four refuseniks of practicality; a truly *glassy* carpentry interface sourced by Shim, gleaning the surfeit of interworld to a honed how-to; a nod of Sifu Renart at his new prentice-cum-project Jaq's keen pleas of could they could they could they build in the stead's outback and could he cannibalise detritus needing cleared from neath the rooms anyways, an amused *for sure*; the providence of a gravity forgiving craftsmanship of a slapdash sort Puk baulked at on first wary glance, quipped at, daggering Jaq's pride to a huff.

Apologies, remonstrations followed, and forgiveness, keen-shifting weeks of friendship.

Yesterday he shanghaied the lad. It was a natural progression.

•

WHY NOT? SAYS Jaq.

Because, says Joi.

Jaq flicks a browned shrivel of apple core off a bollard into the river, gives a petulant *fuff*. Don and Shim are strolled on ahead down the Left Bank esplanade, talking of Carthage, Hiroshima, Tempe, oblivious in the throng of tourists and hawkers, Shim passing one of the beers for the sauna to Don.

The cadres met up after a visit home as brief as Jaq could keep it, dutiful son checking in on Maman and Papa Cartier, answering phatic interrogations with sheepish assurances that, yes, all was Bristol fashion with Sifu Renart, more stanced down on his haunches though, to the scruffle of Diogenes's tummy, as the dog, no doubt, meted only fair. The honour of his presence, as his Maman hies it wryly, lasted all of half an hour before the scarper to hook up with his cohort, meeting Shim and Don in the Old Town, Joi at the docks just back off the barque his old man had him slogging all spring on. Jaq knew Shim and Don would be cliqued, but was hoping Joi would have a hanker on for after the beery steam and plunge pool, bored to blissom from his stint away. They could hit the Jardins Rochester, the Libertine Meadow where anything goes. Knew he was pipe-dreaming—*saved as a geist*, said Shim, shaking her head—but still... it's a scunner.

At ease with his kinsey of two-going-on-three in adolescent flex, Jaq spent last summer fankled with Don and Shim in the quilted snug of the treehouse, the blood cadres, even Joi for some of it, a tangle of limbs and lips, exploring quirks of yen and trigger. Each already, of course, a wide-minded polymath of tumblespace cocks and cunnies, boobs and butts, erudite in the razzmatazz of show-off peers and hoary old freaks casting fetishes to goggle young lewdsters, make them kench and retch. Jaq a caster himself indeed, of some ambit indeed, followed in Xanthe, Kasei, Tempe, all over. Been teasing the touchscreen walls since he could.

So, hardly ingénues letting the interworld inside for the first, dancing in the carnival for the first. But. Debuting fleshwise, versing each other in the fondle, not just vision, of girth and gape, hood and nubbin. Best was the sandwich, Jaq in the middle, crushed and exploding, fucker of Shim, fuckee of Don—lavish maybe, but basking in other's regard is his craft, his vocation. Hence his prenticing to Renart; a pataphysician needs the skill of brazenry in any project, and Jaq is nothing if not brass.

Only... Don and Shim are swans for each other these days, and Joi has no hanker at all, refuses point-blank to tweak himself even for the propriety of ludic empiricism. And Jaq's hanker is well stoked.

It's the scientific method, says Jaq, theory and experiment. We could be proving each other right now.

No, says Joi.

Why not?

Because.

Because why?

It's as Joi rolls his deadlights to the skies that Jaq's sigh turns his doldrum gaze to clock two arrivals daunering off the Gunnison Pier, skirted by Don and Shim who disappear behind these dazed exotics, her and him in startle of synthe filligree trews and jerkins unbuttoned, hight Ana and Puk Massinger on the New Davenport barque's manifest, embarked at Gunnison Airport, hailing from Tempe afore, from Earth afore that, as if the Geister garb weren't advert of such; she's a freelance academic, pataphysicist on contract at Erehwyna's Hovendaal Institute; he's her kid brother emancipated to her custody after—

Jaq clocks the note of his query's dint on the brother's face, the turn of eyes afluster at casual gandering, savvies sharp that it's a jostle for the Earther more than any milling of Erehwyna's Left Bank clamjamfry in tourist season, bites it back. He's framing a sorry and intro when the backdint in his own nous tells of gandering in return, a swatch at name and tumblespace, at casts.

A pause.

Puk Massinger cocks his head at him from down the street, eyebrows raised to stance: *oh my*.

Jaq actually blushes. For the first time, like, ever.

•

A SOFT BREEZE rustles leaves of linden and oak, a susurrus. Jaq pulls the cap from his head, scruffs hair. Up anchors and away.

What Jaq games to a port behind him: onyx-slated roof jumble of Erehwyna, town-state on the banks of the Erehwyreve, which flows off north by northwest between Gunnison and Mikkel-Nikolai, to the five mile wide Rio Reullvale, to Harmakhis Bay and New Davenport's glass urbanity; jumbled Erehwyna with its second century Old Town stone stockade crumbled to park wall of the Jardins Rochester here, co-opted into conurbation and bastion conversions there; closer, the southern outbelt of subrural steads woven with asphalt trails through woodland; the gimbaled spires that rise high over foliage, gracile powermill vanes wheeling slowly to the susurrus and the sun; closer, Sifu Renart's rough stead of adobe, overgrown ever-open gates into the horseshoe courtyard where prentice Jaq postures like a Harlequin for Picasso; closer, the brambling border of the stead, a copse as crowd at his imagined docks, thin trail blazed weavy through it, to be run as a buck darting fast, leaping dead branch and straythorn tripwire, to be run as a pickpocket dodging artful to his den, soles slapping off a springboard gangplank, monkeyboy arcing through lithe Martian gravity to catch the rope ladder and freck his way up, trimmed in pirate slops and élan, barefoot.

Cocked to an idle weighting on one heel, he drapes an arm over a branch, other hand shading fire opal eyes for a peer to the horizon. Time is a volume, measured in ticks and yonks, two moments of the same stint condensed by different acuities of shift, charged to different intensities of span. If shift is gradient, span is breadth. If shift is attack, stint is sustain. With the shifts of the end of spring, this month of Qof was a mountain Jaq has come tumbling down to find himself beyond it.

Ahoy of him, the future is another world, Earth, growing its roots ever deeper into ever deeper soil.

Through the canopy engulfing his den, a susurrus whispers.

No, *the* susurrus whispers.

No...

•

SUSURRUS WHISPERS THROUGH the grass and gorse, godling of the Martian wind, gene-spliced tyke of Zephyros and Ares. His story needs no Ovid, tells itself in the rustle of striplings and flowers he loves, the tale that he is: a zygote collaged from: spermatazoa flensed to nuclear caducei; a mathematical transform by the Fréres Fourier, Jean and Charles, flip of an axis changing Y to X; and the egg from which Eros hatched, is always hatching, offered up blithely to a god of war gone broody, Ares a sharper marksman than any brat with bow and arrow, no more to be argued with than the groundling Renart in a frum.

It's all quite impossible, of course, temporally, physically, logically, but quite viable pataphysics as pioneered by Burroughs and Braque, in scissors and paste. Susurrus can't exist, but he doesn't *have* to exist in the sibilance of air swirling soft through foliage, no more than the number six exists in the perianth of a daffodil. No more than the colour carnelian exists in the lad in the treehouse built within Philemon and Baucis, Jaq Cartier of Erehwyna, the back of whose neck Susurrus tickles just to see the shudder of spine.

Jaq turns now, satchel in one hand, cap in the other, towards the door of the treehouse. Susurrus slides inside his open doublet to tickle skin, a thumb of air brushing nipple. He approves wholeheartedly of the lovers' scheme, even if the fleshling is mixing the piratical and the Peloponnese in his imagination, matelots and myrmidons. Susurrus wouldn't be here if it weren't for such antics.

Twisty it is, that the solitary hold-out in a pantheon of lad-lovers should be the first to sire with a stud. Not the king of lightning with his fetching garçon fetched by eagle. Not the mouse with his flower cut down by discus, nor the ocean with his jambalaya boy rebuilt with bionic ivory shoulder. Not the lion-skinned circus strongman with his sailor led AWOL by the nymphs. The hoplite in helm and cuirass was the first co-father, his cold and arid wilds gentled warm by Zephyros newly arrived from Earth with the fleshlings. As the little bald monkeys danced out across the red churl, swaddled in their white romper suits, driving tin can coracles on jets and wheels, building geodesic domes, Zephyros slipped out among them, tentative, questing.

And we met, your further and I, he'd tell young Susurrus as he hoiked the lad into the air, whirled him upside down, squealing—

We met, your feather and I, burly Ares would butt in, huchling the infant from his grip and twirling to set him aright upon the soil—

Atop Olympus Mons of course, they'd say together, where else?

And it was love at first sight? says Susurrus.

And it was love at first sight.

•

THE FIELD MOUSE scurries over Puk's rondeling palms, shy dun but as sprack in whiskers and scamper as Puk's eyes, those aureate-flecked amber irides around wide pupils, blinking to Jaq and back. *Apodemus sylvaticus*, Puk says, Apple by name. Cross-fertilised derivation from the fruit and deity, Apollo Sminthius, who was worshipped as a mouse god on Tenedos.

He lies prone on the quilt that rugs the inside of the treehouse, clothes shucked in a corner. The quilt is a patchwork of baizes, every nap and hue of meadow, pasture, field, orchard, a tablecloth of green fields, just a little rumple here and there. Puk upon it is a deep shade of sard, smooth, almost as swarth as Joi and Don, raised on elbows so the inverse arch of his back slopes sigmoid down to pert plum rump, an arse made for tarse he proudly claimed to Jaq as they hung out in Market Square first day they met proper, Puk having taken the Erehwyna native up on the offer of a Sherpa of the city, the wandering's end wound up with Jaq lounged on the Cenotaph plinth at the angle of late afternoon, back to the brass plaque, earning scowls from passing grand dames in silk kaftans, Puk posed in front of him like Peinte's

Orpheus, twisting to display said posterior and peer back over his shoulder as if to admire it himself, Diogenes as a pup curling to catch his tail. It was indeed comely, Jaq agreed then, not the full girly plump of an Antinous but a cute convexity, fit to his neat hips.

Now in the naked ephebic flaunt of it, it seems perfect.

Jaq crouches to flick his Monmouth onto the pile of clothes, a cherry of vermilion wool on the leathery, silvery grey.

His legs kicked up at the knee, Puk's feet dangle in the air, crossing at the ankles, uncrossing. Earthen as the mouse, packaged compact of frame but snug rather than squat, he's a wildcat to Jaq's cheetah, withy to his lissome. Jaq was strung to this for the first few days they hung, unsure if his stance of appetence was maybe clueless Martian cock-fluffed just by the exotic, the Earther as Other. There's no erasing the centuries of abjection under the Xanthean Dominion, the scorning of those who quit civilisation to rebuild Earth, prodigal fathers of a new frontier.

Jaq slumps the satchel on the floor, flicks the flap open, roots.

There is no utopia. It is a fact of how the word *stunted* works now, of the scatter of its import—*primitive, puerile, puritan*—that an Eryhwynan stance is like to pivot at Puk's head-and-shoulders brevity, whether the tuning is sensed or not. To an Erehwynan, the Earther's undersize can't help but signal inhibition of growth, signal a barbarian as buttoned-up in stance as in style, by Geister rhetoric of weak flesh transcended in death. Jaq is not immune, even as a stancer of talent, even savvy since his own Phobian roots, advertised in cinnabar freckles speckling jasper nose, shoulders and forearms, carry heritage of hate from a century when his refugee forebears were all *criminal, cunning, capricious*. He knows of bigotry and the sneaky fetish too.

Doesn't it smack of dodgy to you, Jaq asked when they were scheming the summer, the whole cultivate the Earther thing?

You *are* thieving me, Puk said and flicked thumbnail on upper teeth. Scallie.

Dirter, said Jaq.

Waveson, said Puk. Fob-filcher.

In the end, Jaq was settled by the facticity of Puk's axial kinsey, as utmost as his linear six, rendering him as sub as homo, and Puk with no more inclination to tweak it than Joi with his hanker. Or as Puk put it: you're the top; lump it. So, they hatched the plot of this summer's shift.

Jaq closes fingers on the waxy orb buried under muslined cheese and bread, lurking down with the jarred Harmakhis olives, the flask of Kasei red. He draws it out with a flourish, an offering.

An apple for Apple, he grins. Or a core for him at least, after you're done.

Puk rolls and hassles upright, scootching cross-legged and staying the mouse in one hand's grasp while he reaches for the Devonshire Quarrenden, small English fruit of French parentage, August seasonal so likely imported from Up North, sweet with a strawberry kick, juicy and crisp, peel crimson as the scratch on the back of Jaq's hand.

Ouch, says Puk with a nod.

Jaq shrugs, which becomes with easy grace a shucking of his doublet, thereafter tossed to the pile.

It is twenty three hours and seventeen minutes since the kidnapping, Joi, Shim and Don assisting in the transparent ruse and transport of the target via Don's skimpod, from the esplanade back to Renart's, whereupon the cadres left Jaq to sling Puck in a fireman's carry and yomp him through the brush, stray spikewire of aculeate smilax snecking the back of a hand thrown out for balance when the abducter stumbled once stepping over a log.

•

SMILAX DOES NOT taste the fleshling's blood, barely notices it; he tromped by her with no more than a touch and that's all she asks. She has no time for suitors in skin and stride, just a sprig of a stint to them and barely any span at all, just shift, shift, shift. She has no time for them in any dimension—does shimmy to the touch of Susurrus though, she must admit. But that's different.

Not that Susurrus is the only idler to ease his way through *Smilax asperi*'s thrawn barricade of spinney. Bees buzz freely among the thicket of spiny greenbrier stems. Beetles trek methodical through the mulch she weaves with rhizome, masses with her prickle and leathery leaf, (cordate, glabrous,) hooking thorns to clamber bark and branch, near ten metres tall in places. Finches hop in and out with a flutter. She is not wholly impenetrable, really only harsher to the fleshlings who have tussled each other into her bindweed thrash, struggled yelping out with vicious scratches from the catbrier's claws to slap at each other's taunt and dodge, to grump sullen and swearing, nurse thin welts beading blood.

She has no time for meat and bone striplings like these anymore, not after how she felt for Krokos. Or didn't. She loved him but he didn't love her. He loved her but she didn't love him. They loved each other but death sundered them. The tales contradict, so it's impossible to say for sure. But it all ended badly, as it tended to in those days; that much is certain. Aphrodite took pity on her as she wept over the flower her boy had become, as thieving Hermes looked away sheepishly. She became a symbol of luckless love, worn only in the garlands of maenads as they danced in frenzies to Dionysus, sacred to the Erinyes who might have been her sisters, born like her of the night. No more flower boys for her.

Susurrus is a different kind of flirt though, fickle as a godling of wind can only be but light and warm as one father, bold as the other. And his is a different kind of love, one that has lasted near as long as this world has now and stayed as fresh somehow, even in his flightiness. It is Susurrus makes her sigh for those days, even though he makes them all sigh.

He does so now, not that the fleshlings would notice, though he might well carry her whispers to their ears.

Of course, while she still thinks of herself as *she*, as Smilax, young nymph of the forests outside Sparta, she is dioecious, and this colony has plants of both sexes, anthers and ovaries. Right now racemes of pedicellate flowers, so pale a green they're almost white, await pollination. She will fruit in the fall, produce bright red berries that have been used to treat syphilis and psoriasis or to flavour root beer with sarsaparilla for sale in soda fountains idyllised in fictive smalltowns of American Antiquity called Sehnsucht and Saudade.

Smilax has many species to her genus, some deciduous, some evergreen.

•

DECIDUOUS, SAYS JAQ.

Evergreen, says Puk.

It is not a bickering, but a game for the newly-enabled: how fast and flexy can you riposte a counter-notion harmonically linked; how loose can you link and still claim harmony? Square binaries are beginner stuff—Jaq would have batted back *quercus*, oak genus defying either/or dichotomy inherent in *deciduous* by coming in both, the phonics of retort sleekity sneaking in a crafty binary in short versus long, velar versus dental plosive at start, but both unvoiced and the wholes, further, rhyming at the end. But still. For this naked cabin boy naïf Jaq has stolen away for a grand voyage into summer, this Geister ephebe he savvies from the guarding set of an arm across lap to have stripped for his return as much to prove his will to become a native as to actually flirt as one... for Puk, unlearned in all the games an Erehwynan kidster would have been playing for Mars years, let alone Earther years, who has only just discovered the rules of Fourier Harmonies in a nosey through the interworld, it is a start.

Not bad, says Jaq. Deciduous, circle.

An easy one for the Earther, with a glassy riposte that will pair with Jaq's and extend his own harmony to the second domain, but Puk scrunches bafflement.

Wait, *circle*? How does that follow *deciduous*? I don't savvy.

How could it *not* follow? says Jaq, more flummoxed yet. Deciduous, circle. And you'd riposte *triangle*.

A crunkle of brow, then: Oh.

Remember, says Jaq, it's not meant to follow *mechanically*.

II

•

Back to the road where Ana's skimpod sits parked, nestled between orchards of the steads either side, Jaq's home is a horseshoe galerie house, architected in the Neo-Helladic style: pale adobe and oak timbers giving a vibe half Shaker, half Tudor; ground-floored with an undercroft that would have once been stables; stairs up, at each serif of the omega layout, to the gallery; the upper floor of habitation an oxbowed Chester Row of French-windowed rooms above; master bedsuite at one end, Jaq's and the study at the other, tabled kitchen opening into armchaired salon between; all of this then, embracing its courtyard like a poor man's Rose Theatre of stalls and one balcony, with Renart leaning left forearm and right elbow on said balcony, leaning jutted jaw on fist, a furrowbrowed Shakespeare directing.

Jaq below in the courtyard is Ariel and Caliban ambling out of slumber into stretches of semaphore gibberish, crushing a deboxed silvery bag raised high with a pinch and suck of nozzle to drain the last citrus tang, the tart taste of Seville sangüina. He is Ariel as ballet dance of basketball, arabesqued to shoot the crumpled bag for basket of bin. He is Caliban pumping his fist in triumph, *hooyah*, then ambling on, guddling in his skivvies to scritch, sniffing fingers.

This is one trail of him, at least. Elsewhere, he is standing awkward, right hand clasping left wrist behind back, toe gimbling the sand, head down, eyes up, bottom lip between teeth, offering apology, excuse. Elsewhere, he is a red lion rampant—no, *saltant* in a hornpipe, dancing around the polished basalt font in the centre of the courtyard. And elsewhere and elsewhere and elsewhere, sauntering, stretching, stancing, everywhere the tracer mirages of his motion scrawling through each other as palimpsest of snail trails. He is the flashlight held by Pablo Picasso, the drumsticks in Gene Krupa's hands, every subject streaming in a photoflash study made by Gjon Mili. He is Stanford's horse Occident, in the zoopraxiscope of Eadward Muybridge, proving the flight in a gallop, hooves airborne when tucked under at the moment of switch from pull of forelegs to push of hindlegs.

He is the project Renart is working on, a confusion of sketches in virtual chalk and charcoal snatched by the pataphysician as studies toward a lucid stance.

He is, of course, also cocky in the unveiling of it all, here in the flesh, leading Puk and Ana in through the iron gates, one closed, the other open and half off its hinges, angled back to scrapyard detritus overgrown by undergrowth outside.

It's a temple of you, says Puk agape. An unholy demented bedlam of a temple of you. I'm jargogled.

Order out of chaos, Renart calls down as if it should be plain, the latent kilter to the clutter of this latter-day Da Vinci's workshop, Vesalius's theatre, Feuillet's studio. He straightens, flicks a hand to sweep the jumble of snapshot shifts away to single-image sprites stowed in the undercroft like alcoved statuary, and heads for the stairs to his right, descends to come greet the visitors.

Puk you've met, says Jaq. This is Ana.

Ana Massinger, she says.

Guy Renart, he says.

An Erehwynan greeting: a clasp of right hand to hip, left hand to shoulder, kiss on the left cheek, kiss on the right cheek. The same for Puk, with a salut and an extra slap of shoulder at the end that sends him after Jaq, who is already half up the stairs, beckoning his new friend to come see his suite.

Was that you in my skivvies? says Puk.

Mine now, says Jaq.

Please, says Renart, come in. Jaq tells me you're at the Hovendaal… and more.

The slightest upcrink to the corner of his lips is met with a smile in Ana's eyes.

I can imagine. My brother's been quite garrulous on our affinities.

A moment of wry amusement is shared in what's unsaid. Ana is pataphysicist to Renart's pataphysician, a snick of a distinction as far as Puk is concerned, between science and art. Not to mention their kinseys. They should obviously, Jaq echoed to Renart, get to know each other.

I suspect, says Ana as they follow the conspirator cupids upstairs, we're the only full heteros they know.

And in the same decade of life, says Renart. Clearly we're meant for each other.

The soft laugh of Susurrus puffs a stray lock of hair across Ana's face, and she tidies it back behind her ear with one hand as, with the other, she hands Renart the bouquet of hyacinth she savvies is customary in the Erehwyna region, where to bring wine on a visit would be considered an insult to the host's choice.

•

A PERENNIAL PLANT, *Hyacinthus orientalis* sprouts from a bulb of three to seven centimetres in diameter. His ligulate leaves like straps, soft fifteen to thirty-five centimetres long, only a few succulent centimetres wide, produced from the basal whorl around a stem growing to between twenty and thirty-five centimetres tall, spiking into a terminal raceme that may bear, in the spring, as few as two, as many as fifty little flowers pointing every which way. Each flower, pendent to suberect, has a funnel-shaped perianth of only ten to thirty-five millimetres, constricted in the middle with the six lobes strongly recurved. Most often purple, the blossoms of Hyakinthos are pollinated by honey bees drawn to his nectar and sweet fragrance, at its strongest now, around eleven at night, as he sits in the vase on the table of Renart's kitchen, taking pride of place among the remnants of the traditional Haft-Sin setting, late in the season for the true spring celebration, but offered by the maestro in the aim of hospitality, to introduce the Massinger siblings to the culture of their new environs.

Hospitality is in the bones here, Jaq said at one point during the evening. It's ossature.

So, in front of Hyakinthos—and reflected in the mirror at his back, propped against the wall and sentried by candles that have all but burned down—there sits what is left of the seven key items: a flask of vinegar as symbol of patience in senescence; a silver dish of red sumac fruit as symbols of the dawn to come; a walnut fruitbowl that still has one apple in it, for health and beauty; a silver dish of garlic bulbs as symbols of medicine; a china plate of dried oleaster fruit, for love; empty bowls that held the wheat germ pudding, sumana, signifying wealth; and a few sprouted mung beans lurking uneaten at the bottom of their ceramic bowl, symbols of rebirth.

Other than this? Each place setting still has its painted egg. The chocolate coins are long since gone, devoured by Jaq, just as the baqlava was polished off by Puk. Nuts; raisins, currants and sultanas; berries: the bowls of healthier fare are also emptied of all but pits and shells, one stray pistachio of which floats in Renart's fingerbowl of rosewater. The leatherbound copy of Haikonnen's *Gilgamesh* that Ana found exquisite in its handsewn craftsmanship was taken with her on their adjourn to the armchairs, now lies on the cushion at her back as she leans forward, pauses to puff her cigar before making a point in a spry debate with Renart that reminds Hyakinthos of Athena and his philator Apollo at their most spirited, how he would lie with his head in Apollo's lap—as Puk lies with Jaq now in the latter's suite, according to the gossipy flutter of the moth batting against the French windows—while the gods argued their dialectic of justice and beauty, and Eros, who was always there whenever he was with Apollo, whispered in his ear, asking with a sly insouciance if they weren't just the same thing anyway, and his domain when it came down to it: passion.

That was before the discus from Apollo's hand was caught by Zephyros in a fit of pique that the braw ephebe wasn't his, brought whipping round in the wrong direction, as the head of Hyakinthos whipped round at Apollo's cry, too late. The next thing he knew, if *knew* is the right word for it, he was a flower, the hyacinth of the ancient Greeks, described by Theophrastus, *Gladiolus segetum*,

Not this flower then. No, Hyakinthos's tale took a peripetaia here on Mars during the Interregnum, when he welked into a crushing melancholia, homesick and miserable that his legend was lost by the fleshlings, along with so much of their past, to discus deaths of light so bright they turned Tempe to sand, to glass, shattered a moon to dust. He wept to Susurrus that the few who knew his name at all inked it under paintings of other flowers. He was forgotten.

The godling of the Martian wind carried the sad tale to his father, Zephyros, who brooded the woe of it. Ares snorted at his pity, stropped at the soppy of it all, but gentle Zephyros, still gritted with guilt over his jealous crime, gleaned a catharsis of his hamartia. Down he swept from Olympus Mons, across the whole surface of the planet, to gather every grain of stance in which Hyakinthos was coded, to lift up the pollen of his soul, as a primitive poet might say, to glimmer it with a breath in his hand, to breeze it everywhere, to fertilise every carpel of every common hyacinth. Seed capsules, fleshy, spherical and tripartite, ripened from the pollinated flowers, split and spilled their diaspores, black grains with a white elaiosome, dispersed by myrmechocory, ants taking the seed back to their burrows, using the elaiosome for food, discarding the remains outside their nest or in a midden within.

Hyakinthos was reborn in the first generation of hyacinths germinating from those seeds, as were the fleshling cultures that surround the Hellas Sea, a joy marked to this day in Erehwyna and beyond by his presence on every table set for vernal visitations. As here and now.

•

PARTICLES, SAYS JAQ.

Waves, says Puk.

A suite: ahoy, a wall of French windows leading out onto the balcony, one opened to the night, to the warm breeze and the sound of cicadas; larboard, a wall with two doors, leading to pisser and scrubber, touchscreen between, mute to bone white; starboard, a wall arrayed with walnut dresser desk in the unornamented Mei style, open shelving and rails built round for clothes and gubbins decidedly unshipshape in the stowage; aft, a touchscreen wall also mute to bone white, with a sleigh bed also walnut, as too the shelf above said bed.

On the shelf above the bed: one glow-in-the-dark yoyo, milky-white with the piss-yellow tinge of fluorescence; one glass hand, sliver of neckchain drooped to weave between pinky and pointer, silver ring dropped on the digitus impudicus, abandoned bling of a whim for trimmings, Jaq has explained, too much hassle in the off and on; one black painted iron spearhead of a broken railing, fleur-de-lis tipped, as some hobo Prospero's sceptre; one white slinky; one hologram diorama, capering sprites of Joi, Don and Shim, figurines in a loop of frolic that shines above its grey plinth. Joi hunkered on haunches, flop of fringe shading eyes as he skins a tab, looks up and clocks it coming just as Don tackles, tumbles them both back, downhill, head over heels over head over heels, and Shim runs in to leap atop the stramash; cut to start.

Particles, says Jaq.

Waves, says Puk.

On the bed, naked: a laze of a Puk reclines on the cushion of Jaq's abdomen, Jaq raised on pillowheap against the headboard, looking down over tousle of crow-black hair that tickles his tum with the upturn of head, to the youth between his legs. They are sard and carnelian figurae on a ground of saffron linen. They are art, inheritors of genetic tinkerings, of chain-reacting Martian ideologies pre-Interregnum, of runaway politics, which is to say ethics, which is to say aesthetics. Humans were not always dark this way and golden-eyed, but have been so since before even the return of Puk's progenitors to desolate Earth. For Puk and Jaq, what they are now is as natural as the recurve bow lineament of an upper lip: Puk's Schytian, cherubic, flesh; Jaq's Avar, ephebic, muscle. As natural as the libidinous mash of such, as the fit of each other's pintle in paw shoved down trews unbuttoned or britches unknotted, as the breaths between liplock to ungarb the pivot of this vast moment, frenziedly ungarb and grab back into kiss, to throw or be thrown onto the bed, to straddle or be straddled, arching to rhythm of rising tempo in the alien grasp, to throb of another rhythm sudden under it, taking over to pulse, Puk spurting first, Jaq squirting in ecstasy at the squeezing buck beneath, and O the spattering of Puk. Collapse to clasp, savouring the shift. And now they lie lazybones, quick-sprouting hanker of their week-long friendship sated. Jaq, curious, broached the subject of Puk's sixer kinsey: hadn't he ever thought to twiddle, to try girls? Which brought them to binaries, male and female, top and bottom, subject and object, charm and strangeness.

Particles, says Jaq.

Waves, says Puk.

Skins stick with sweat where they press, are silk to the stroke where dried by Susurrus—Puk's shoulders smoothed by Jaq's palms, Jaq's thigh brushed by the backs of Puk's fingers. The mingle of scents animal and ammonial hits notes familiar and foreign to both, inversely, each recognising the aroma of their own jism, savouring the novelty of the other's. To Jaq, Puk is almond, vanilla, bacon. To Puk, Jaq is oranges, chocolate, cheese.

They settle on helices, spiraling springs of existence in stint, span and shift, the three dee of time. The slinky stretched becomes a closed circle or ongoing undulation depending on which angle of eye you lose, which dee you're not seeing. Imagine it horizontal and laterally bisected by Edwin Abbott Abott's Flatland and you'd have a series of dots arranged as leafs alternate on a stem—left, right, left, right—as footprints in sand, seemingly disconnected but entirely of a unity if one only grasps the other dimensions.

•

The Crete of the juvenile Zeus is where Krokus was born, *Crocus sativus*, as a sport of his wild precursor, created by intensive selection for the slender inch-long crimson stigmas dried to make saffron, red spice for paella and bouillabaise, golden dye for the robes of a Minoan snake-goddess, Buddhist monks. Greek hetaerae used saffron in their scented waters and ointments, perfumes and potpourris, mascaras and medicines, offerings at the shrine of Persephone, who was picking his purple blossoms when abducted, whose return he announced via a kindred species of his genus, bright golden *Crocus chrysantheus.* At first, Demeter shook with fury to see their gaiety, having ruled that naught should flourish till her daughter be returned.

But the Kore is coming, he said, and the ground split, and Persphone rose from Hades, and the world renewed.

On Earth, as sterile as he was sacred, Krokus had to be cultivated by the manual crack of a season's starchy brown corm, less than two inches in diameter, into all his sundry cormlets, up to ten of them forming even as the old corm that fed him through his aestivation shriveled, as he shot up maybe five to eleven leaves, nigh vertical, maybe a foot high, budding inverted purple teardrops in the fall, to blossom late, lazybones October lover that he is, unfolding a cup of six petals shaded light as lilac, violet, mauve, three yellow anthers furred with pollen, and those three stigma of blood.

On Earth, he was precious; they remade him here on Mars, grafted the genes of other species of his genus into his chromosomes, unleashed him to grow wild again as he hadn't done for a fistful of millennia. He's no longer quite the same Krokus killed by the discus of Hermes, dropped to his knees from the mishap, blood dripping down over doe-eyes that sought his lover's face with stunned confusion—*Am I to die now?*—blood dripping to splash in the soil, each drip sprouting a bloom with the red of his mortality staining those precious stigmas.

But maybe he never was. Wasn't that Hyakinthos anyway, and the discus of Apollo? Wasn't his tale to do with Smilax wasting away for the love he squandered in the hunt, Aphrodite's prayer to Artemis damning him for his callow disdain? It's all a bit dreamy still, bleared with slumber.

Still, Krokus is awakening now, in a patch of feral rock garden on the edge of a stead inhabited again, these last few years, by fleshlings. Curious for news of them, he is pushing up to the brush of Susurrus across the tip of his shoots, the godling wind barely touching, like some cat sashaying slow at the very extent of reach, just close enough for fingertips to feel the soft of fur. The tease.

Facing the gates—and facing the sun, so happily facing the sun, albeit with boorish brambles threatening his back—he has a good spot for the sideshow, stretches up from the earth eager to know: has the one of blunt shift who arrived first started gardening? maybe pruned that dishevelry at the side of the gates? is the other still around, the one of keen shift who hurricaned through the scrapwood of the undercroft? any sign he might bring a similar reckoning to the brambles? does he know, zesty hotspur that he is, apparently, according to the tales brought back by Susurrus, that I was an aphrodisiac in the bath of Cleopatra, salve in the bath of Alexander?

He wasn't cherished just for his rarity. Krokus is the paragon of spice, herald of hanker and fettle. Here on the cusp of summer, he is only just awakening, but he can feel the shift of the season in him, and O if he were a fleshling again, how he would yawn and flex.

His name is older than the Greek language.

•

RENART GRASPS THE asperity of blood orange from the stancing of Jaq, torques it to scry the overflow into suck of cheeks, correlates with the simultaneous backflex of shoulders as under a chiropractor's knead. A moment of deliciation to be drawn out, a moment of gusto—he capsules and logs it, another note in the project that is Jaq.

The project: where Kristeva situates the abject in a conceptual space between the subject and the object, alive and yet not, that which was once us but is no longer, Davenport turns this inside out with the notion of the *project*, that which was once *not* us but *is now*. Objectivity, subjectivity, projectivity: it was a natural progression. Early critics confused Davenport's new paradigm of perspective with the narcissist child undifferentiated from its environs, ungrasping that the world is not the sphere of one's desires, a handmaid holding a mirror as extension of self—the state, in short, before one truly knows there is a not-me. No, Davenport said, projectivity requires anagnorisis of one's own agency, is the recognition precisely of one's distinction, how the echoes and resonances engrave.

As within, so beyond.

The soft toy of the thumbsucking years, identity jounced into it with every giggle. The project begins where possession becomes attribute. As Zeus's lightning is Zeus unleashed into the world, so the child's teddy bear *is* the child.

The bedsuite walls, wearing our infant enthusiasms as reliquary touchscreens, self strewn over its surfaces in images of stars, human or celestial, the constellations of desire. The difference between object and project is that between house and home. With the first red ochre hand print, the Paleolithic cave ceased to be just a cave, became the inside of our head turned out.

Our attitudes, mouthed not by us but in a friend's wrangle of impulse or opinion, as they conjure our voice to play the angel of their better nature, their imp of the perverse, imagining the argument we'd make. As we imprint ourselves on others, we render them our project too, extend ourselves into their thoughts, their dreams, their skins; it is, of course, always reciprocal.

The pad and turf, a little studio apartment and terrain of streets surrounding, inscribed with our encounters and exchanges. Actions ephemeral in the stint of time persist in the shift of it.

The ouvre of statuary, cinema, simcasts blossoming out into the interworld. All art is the project.

It sounded, said Ana—when he dropped into the Hovendaal last week to see what she was gleaning from his mass of stancings, Jaq's, his own, a little of Puk's, and found her zombied by an umpteen hour stint of hard analysis through the night, followed her shamble in to scope in wry recognition of vocational ardour every touchscreen wall of her office a scroll of diagrams and data, and dawdled while she wrapped up close enough to an encapsulation, until he could cluck her away to an unwinding over beer and cigars in a tabac off Boulevard Max Keirinckx, where she came alive again in blether—it sounded as if he *ought* to savvy fine well how all of this, all their environs and actions in them, could be the substrate of agencies simply less secure, in the epistemological sense, more insecure in the eigenstate sense, than fleshly humans. He does find her work fascinating, he told her, but has to admit she loses him with the mathematics. His own understanding of projectivity is terribly pragmatic.

Renart flicks a finger to open the same infospace store he bumped her, leafing through a sheaf of sprite sheets sigiled *prudence*. Not the thickest sheaf, natch, given a project such as Jaq, but for all the wildling stances grinning pride in his abandon, Jaq can be subtler than, Renart suspects, he savvies of himself. He finds a note, tweaks it out and twirls it open: Jaq in a tabac with his mates, huddling in to plot with them, head popping up for a scope, tenty of Puk returning from the pisser, then down again; moving his beer aside to lean forward, arms crossed.

We write our souls into the substance of the world, Davenport said in the antiquity before *stance* replaced such fancies as *soul* or *sign*, his lecture to a few hundred symposiasts cached and unearthed down centuries and between worlds, surviving as if to prove his point, dug from a dead library, palimpsested memory gleaned to a reconstruction of avatar in cyberspace—a ceramic grace in the rendering, Renart thought when he viewed it whiles ago, the linear elegance of an ochre-on-black athlete limned on a clay potsherd, but as a surface rather than a contour. Volume as form, unfleshed, the avatar seemed a cartoon stood against even the sketchiest sprites of the day—and this before the Tetsuo Interface was cultivated. Stood against the stancings of today... well, he has a note of Jaq shown it for the first, boggling derision: That's *yanked*.

Something to be said for the clarity though, Renart mulls. Aegean, Minoan, Cycladic.

Il y a des imbéciles qui définissent mon œuvre comme abstraite, Brâncuşi said, pourtant ce qu'ils qualifient d'abstrait est ce qu'il y a de plus réaliste, ce qui est réel n'est pas l'apparence mais l'idée, l'essence des choses.

There is a simplicity to Jaq's stances that might be modeled better in a single Brâncuşi bronze than in all these detailed simulacra.

•

He left you on the doorstep? says Ana. Puk!

We were squiffy. Oh, the boulanger was by. I got a baguette. He says if you want an order just dint him.

I... thanks. Seriously, he left you out here all night? *Puk!*

It's nearly summer. And I can kip anywhere, like Diogenes. Not my Diogenes, the original, well, my Diogenes too. I ate some of the baguette, sorry. It's a custom—the doorstep, I mean.

Erehwynan? I don't glean any—wait, you mean Geister? Did he fib you that? The sleekit...

No, a sixer custom, from way aft.

Skinsacks for burning. Just... get in here; you look deadmeat. Yes, through there. Puk! Mind the crates; haven't even begun to unpack. *Puk Massinger*! Yes, *you*.

Mhmm? Salut, Jaq, sis—*ow!* What was that for?

You have to ask?

Seriously, it's peachy. It was my fancy really—ooh, stiff. Can I filch some juice, pretty Puk?

Got some pamplemousse in the chiller, ouais? It's nifty how you hie it that here. Pamplemoussy juicy.

Save me now, I give up. Jaq, if you need a drop, I'm taking the skimpod out...?

I'm on a freeday. Puk and I were going to hang.

So, sister of mine, you're swinging by Casa Renart then?

He has some skinny on the local phantoms, echoes in his stancings, could be—don't make those eyes at each other.

See, I *savvied* they'd be simpatico—*ow!* Quit it.

You: behave. And you: just... for the love of your ancestors, just don't let him jump you off a cliff.

It *was* my—ooh, thanks. It *was* my fancy. Honest.

For sure. You're too good for him, you know? Take care. You too, Pukey.

Banana.

Ciao, Ana.

...

Oh, I got you some bread from the boulanger.

Mmmm! Manna from the heavenly. That's...
I ate some.

III

•

Metis, Susurrus murmurs through the open French window of Renart's study, primal Titan of cunning, was glurped down as a fly by Zeus, the king of gods fraught with a prophecy that any sprat got on her would be grander than the father, fraught that he himself might sire a usurper sharp to do to Zeus what Zeus had done to Kronos—maybe even what Kronos had done to Uranus before. Which is to say, scythe the primogenitor's bollocks off and hurl them to the leaping dolphins of the sea, to the spume from whence scalloped Aphrodite sprang—not as some Botticelli damsel, but as a spindrift passion crashing over rock, a naked beauty left crouched, shedding kelp as she rises, looking up to the whorl of scattered gulls, transforming to doves in the gaze of her pearl eyes. Ashore, on the cliffs above, spatters of loinblood on soil had similarly seeded furies, giants, the Meliae of the Manna-ash trees, *Fraxinus ornus*, who would one day raise Zeus on their honey in the hills of Crete, in a cave that was, at least, not the belly of Kronos.

It was Metis who gave Zeus the potion to poison his father's cup, make him vomit Hades and Poseidon from that belly, a canny dame indeed, and mother of a future majesty surpassing all it came from, so said Prometheus.

At which Zeus chewed his beard, brooding on nemesis as his own reign turned to the tyrannical, until the scheme struck: to dare Metis, who was by now his first wife, to metamorphose to a bluebottle if she could, whereupon he snatched her from the air and swallowed her, like a monkey with a grub, num num num. *Urp.* (This is how Susurrus was told it by his fathers, with a flapple of fingers in the clap of hand to mouth, the bug-eyes of a fervent bug-eater. Susurrus giggled at it every time.)

But the sprat was already begat, was born and grew inside the belly of Zeus, spent her childhood dreaming of discoveries beyond, even as Metis clambered up into the god-king's noggin to mine the metal of his mountainous skull, smelt it and hammer a helm of bronze for Athena, goddess of wisdom, who was finally unleashed by Hephastaean chisel and mallet, at Zeus's own agonised pleas, bursting full-grown from a cranium cracked by migraines, madness. Fleshlings would later shilly-shally that the prophecy spoke of a son, of course, not this doting daddy's girl who was but his word made virgin flesh by allegory, the sword and scales of his judgement. Patriarchal piffle. Zeus surrendered his lightning on the Aeropagus the day the Furies let Orestes live, kept only his thunder for two thousand years of petulant denial, stomping off to Rome, Jerusalem, Mecca to steal an empty throne, play wizard behind the veil, until eventually Athena strode into his office, put him over her knee and spanked the unjovial boor back to the honey-fed towhead brat he once was, Zeus Velchanos of Minoan Crete, a long-haired youth sat in a tree with a cockerel in his lap.

All this from the swallowing of a fly! says Susurrus.

Renart is having none of it, paying no mind at all to the godling's rustle of pages on his desk. Wisdom in a fly is the last notion he can credit right now; flies are fuckwittery on wings. Why, for as long as there have been wide-open windows, Renart has not an iota of doubt, from before even those windows were glazed most like, bluebottles have been buzzing around some narrow-eyed ponderer's room, buzzing this way and that, by ear, at the back of head, buzzing to rattle the window and away again, sighted against ceiling, lost among clutter, buzzing everywhere but out of that window, everywhere but away from the—for cock's sake!—from the sworn and obstinate stalk of muttered malevolence, from the swipe of makeshift swatter and sweep around to further swat-swipe-swish, from paroxysms of frustrated thrashing at... this dipteraic dipstick... this calliforaic cretin... this fat farty *moron* of a bumbleturd.

Hallo?

Ana calls from the courtyard below again: Hallo?

As Renart steps out onto the balcony, folded sheaf of notes still in hand, the fly buzzes past him and away. Susurrus follows, down past Ana where she stands at the gate, devilling a little dust around her feet before he slips off into the brush beyond.

•

YOU SAVVY HOW they did it, right? says Jaq.

A poke of dried jujubes in one hand, he pops one of the little fruits in his mouth.

Puk savvies fine, natürlich, his PAN linking into the date-plum leaf he twirls by its petiole as Jaq leans back against the pillar. Puk savvies the how and why and when and which of the terraforming of this planet, just as he savvies that the geodesic dome of the Wilmot Arboretum in the Jardins Rochester, their first stop on today's adventure, replicates the aluminum and perspex Climatron of Missouri Botanical Gardens in San Louis, USA, the Earth's first fully climate-controlled greenhouse, fifty three metres in diameter, twenty one metres high, two thousand two hundred and forty five panes of Plexiglas with a small neo-classical pavilion—which really just means two white marble colonnades—as a folly at the heart of it, raised for picturesque effect and outlook, with a sweep of steps down to ponds and plantings, replicas of which steps Puk now sits on, eyeballing the Martian whose cache of tumblespace casts kept him up half the night after that first encounter. He could reel off the technicalities of the ancient and ongoing transformation, just as he could reel off every detail of Jaq's exhaustive profile and the gleaned history beyond, all the facts and tracks of Jaq.

Even the idlest twinge of curiosity here is a thyrsus driven in the earth, milk and honey of specifics bubbling up out of the interworld in response, words and images, even now: perchlorate and electrolysis;

ammonium and methane; orbital and statite; core and convection.

The arch of an eyebrow though, the sly innocence of a smile, nudges the question to another drift: invitation. Arms folded and legs crossed in his casual lean, Jaq casts the question as a fishing line flicked light through the air, glinting like the lack of guile, the absolute lack of guile, in his eyes.

Puk bites.

OK, he asks. How did they do it?

Smoke and mirrors, says Jaq. Magnets too!

Puk flicks the leaf at him.

It's true, says Jaq. Look it up.

•

Nymphaea lotus, Egyptian White Water Lily.

Not related to Liliacaea, the true lily, this aquatic perennial of the Nymphaea genus grows up to forty-five centimetres in height. Leaves are peltate, with a radial notch from the circumference to the petiole, forming pads that float upon the water, which it prefers clear and warm, still and slightly acidic. She takes her name from the white blossoms, sometimes tinged with pink, which rise above the surface, opening at night, closing in the morning.

Though known also as Tiger Lotus or White Lotus, she is also unrelated to the Nelumbo genus, the lotus of China and India; rather, this is the lotus of ancient Egypt, where she was cultivated, where she signified strength, power, the number one thousand. The Egyptians extracted perfume from her, made funerary garlands and temple offerings. Many women simply wore her flowers for their beauty.

This would suggest that she is not the lotus of Greek legend, who began her life as the maiden Lotis, else all those Egyptians should have met the same sad fate as Dryope, who was turned into a poplar for plucking her flower. Else all the sands of Egypt should have been transformed to one great forest.

•

THE FOLIAGE IN the Arboretum's thick enough. No one will see. Besides, like they'd bat a lash if so, says Jaq. It's naught they couldn't snoop if they wist it. That's what the hylenet *means.*

His doublet dangles in one hand, the other poised over his britches' drawstring. Just one sharpish snapshot of a stance, he wants, the two of them kissing in the folly, skin to skin, framed in marble and vine. Why not? All the tourist couples do it here, like they once threw lire coins in the Trevi Fountain, released tealight balloons from the top of the Pierian Tower, clicked a lover's padlock on the Pont des Arts. It'll be a jape. See, there's even a bench for togs.

Puk can't. No, really. No, he *savvies* it's not like Earth, and, yes, he's the one suggested the Jardins Rochester in the first place, and was gabbling on about fresh air fornication all the walk, but now... yes, he savvies it's silly. It's just... different—oh, and now they just got a courtesy dint from the old couple benched down by the water lily pond, terribly Xanthean about their inadvertent eavesdrop, offering inattention as an Erehwynan offers wine; it must be awkward for an Earther and all, what.

See? says Jaq, then clocks the point in a double take: the poke of jujubes in a waving hand, Puk flapping in a loop, self-conscious that he's self-conscious that he's—

Look, Jaq says, pointing, and—as Puk turns his head toward nothing—plants a kiss on his cheek. Dips fingers. A baffling surprise is blinked, smiled.

What was that f—?

Jaq pops a jujube in the open mouth.

Zen sneak attack, he says. Tell you what; togs on, cool?

I know it's daft, chews Puk as Jaq draws him in.

Ah, husht.

•

Nymphaea caerulea, Egyptian Blue Water Lily.

Her leaves are peltate, twenty-five to forty centimetres across, with a radial notch from the circumference to the petiole, forming pads that float upon the water. She takes her name from the mauve or cerulean or blue-white blossoms, ten to fifteen centimetres in diameter, shading to pale yellow in the centre, which rise above the surface, opening in the morning, closing early for the night, late afternoon.

Her rhizomes are edible, as Isis herself is said to have informed humanity. Psychoactive, sedative, like the mandrakes and poppies she was often rendered with in Egyptian art, as in a bas-relief in the tomb of Tutankhamun where her petals were also scattered freely, she might well be imagined the lotus of the Odyssey's lotus-eaters. But this Sacred Blue Lily, as she is also known, is not a woman transformed to plant; rather the metamorphosis ran the other direction. Rising and falling with the sun, this is the cosmogonic blossom out of which stepped leonine Nefertem, He Who is Beautiful.

•

Jaq is a jaguar in the jungle of the Arboretum, or might be if the freckles dotting his shoulders and forearms were spots, if the jaguar were carved in carnelian but could still somehow pace, leisurely in ease of stone dominion, an apex predator of blood, amber and fire. A shock of sunlight for a mane—heading more to mohawk. Puk is mixing up his cats; he doesn't care.

It's not warped the way he'd think, Puk is explaining. On Earth. Even growing up in a Heartland canton. They haven't fixed kinseys for fifty years now. Shit, the one time he got hassle as a sixer, for getting tender with his squeeze at a wake, well, it was the doctor himself, about as hardcore a Geister as they come, who flamed the maggots to a crisp, scorched them to ash with a rant on the unreason of prejudice.

Puk recalls his Da late on the scene, the handshake from a man who could barely broach without venom the Geisters he'd forsworn. Doesn't mention it.

What's warped, he says, it's that... it's like anyone being a sixer reminds them of kinseys, of hankers, the whole *mire of being meat*. I never got that.

Jaq looks up from the path they stroll, his gaze of golden eyes serene, balancing query in his knitted brows. Patient.

I used to jabber Ana's head hollow about Mars. *Why can't we live in a civilised world?* I was a puke. *On Mars you can hanker how you want.*

Jaq lays a hand on his shoulder, runs it down his back, a stance of comfort for sorrows unspoken, skirted. For a moment, Puk is sure he's about to ask, fraught that he's about to ask. The shift that brought him here is still so keen.

You're here now, says Jaq simply.

•

THERE IS NO utopia, only the ocean named as such, on Mars, and Khadir's novel titled after it, epic of seven ships sailing from the verdant isle of Mie in its white seas, carrying food from a temple that sits at the edge of a spring, in the shadow of a tooba tree; epic of that fleet's sixteen-day-long journey east, to the northern tip of the Phlegra Montes scissioned from the mainland but for the Isthmus of Hurqalya, to relieve besieged Nakojaabad's twin emerald cities of Jabarsa and Jabalqa.

I didn't savvy your ambit, says Ana browsing the bookcases of Renart's study while the pataphysician flicks through capsuled stancings to corrade the promised skinny. When Jaq said you were vaunted I didn't savvy just how high, wasn't until I gandered you... Stancers aren't exactly feted on Earth.

Ambit's a thorny stance in itself, says Renart, something Jaq's still to learn, bless him. The glassiest stancer flenses show.

Ana slides Khadir's *Utopia* back into place between Kafka and Kinsey.

I thought it was *all* show, she says.

Only in the shallows, says Renart. Really it *should* be medicine, affective orthopaedics. I'm hoping Puk might shift Jaq to a glint of that actually.

He capsules the last of the gleanings with a twirl of thumb, dints it to her, all the echoes of the local phantoms.

Here we go, he says.

•

Nymphaea nouchali, Red and Blue Water Lily.

A diurnal and nonviviparous plant with roots and stems submerged, leaves partly so, partly rising above the surface, with a spread of between one and two metres, each round leaf about twenty centimetres, crenellate with undulating edges, green on top with a darker underside.

The flower has four or five sepals and thirteen to fifteen angular petals, usually violet blue, edged in red, though some varieties are best described as purple, mauve or fuchsia. The cup-like calyx has a diameter of eleven to fourteen centimetres and a star-shaped appearance from above, hence the flower is known also as the Blue Star Water Lily or simply as the Star Lotus.

In the Ayurvedic medicine of India, it was known as ambal, used to settle the stomach. In Sri Lanka, it was said that when the Buddha died this flower was one of a hundred and eight signs that sprung up in his footsteps, blossoming wherever he had walked.

•

Up close, sat on the stone wall that borders the lily pond, the scent is heady, a musk of nectar and swamp. Rutting fairies, Puk fancies, a sparkling unicorn tannery. Not that the water of the pond is stagnant, but it's earthy with nutrients, hints of the fetid under the fragrant, sweet as banana but edged as dark to the nose as the still surface is to the eye. He taps a fingertip on the surface; the ripple bobs a stray date-palm leaf.

I just can't wrapple that they used to twiddle kinseys like that, says Jaq. Here... if you're a one, sure, you might wist to go three for a bit, or even six, just to taste it; and a doctor—a physician, I mean, not Earther doctor—he can twiddle you in a tick; but stancing it ethics is just creepy.

Hands wild in the air articulate his flummox.

It's not even *logic,* fixing it as one. Two or five, I can wrapple—that's just flex with a penchant, versatile with a specialty—but one is half-blind. Why would you nix your options like that—?

A blink from the sixer.

—unless you're going expert I mean you could be going expert cause lots of folk do that here that's not weird at all I don't mean...

Sharp backtrack, says Puk. Don't fret. I savvy you don't savvy, bonobo boy.

Jaq shrugs. Halfways maybe, he says. A jaguar doesn't change its dots. What?

Puk peers into his eyes but there's no mischief there, just an honest blink: *what did I say?*

I was just thinking about jaguars, says Puk.

A hand out, palm up, Harlequin presenting their environs.

Um... *jungle,* says Jaq.

•

Ziziphus lotus, THE Lotus Jujube tree.

An aculeate shrub of the buckthorn family, reaching a height of two to five metres. Foliage is deciduous and appears at the end of spring, the ovate leaves about five centimetres long, glabrous with a thin shiny cuticle, a trident of veins prominent at the base. She was known as the sidr in Arabic, a name which she shared with her evergreen cousin, *Ziziphus spina-christa* or the Christ's Thorn Jujube, from which Yeshua's garland of thorns was made.

Her yellow flowers are generally pentamerous, though four, six or seven petals may be observed. Inconspicuous at five millimetres in diameter, the jujube flower was nonetheless worn in the hats of Himalayan men, its sweet smell said to make teenagers fall in love.

A dark yellow globose drupe usually containing two seeds, her fruit is likewise small, one to one and a half centimetres in diameter, but edible fresh or dried. The whole plant is mucilaginous, so the lotus jujube or nabk is of a similar character to the common jujube, soothing the throat, soothing the nerves too, according to Chinese medicine.

Were she the lotus of myth, she might, even from the seeded flesh of the last dried jujube now being munched in Puk's mouth, wish she were here in all her slickly prickly glory to have eased the Earther to the naked kiss his suitor sought, perhaps let drop a little inconspicuous flower or two as the lovers brushed against her, let the blossoms tumble down to lie unnoticed in Jaq's flaxen scruff of hair or on Puk's shoulder, to knit their love with her aroma. But she is neither the Lotis of legend nor here at all now, the last chew of jujube swallowed, paper poke passed back from Puk to Jaq, who scrumples a rummage of fingers, finds it empty, aye, and blasé Puk with hands in jerkin pockets sauntering on, detritus dealt with.

Oi, grumps Jaq.

Perhaps there is no need of her aroma here.

•

A ROBUST ARABICAN scent conjures Colombia and Bourbon, Harar and Java.

You'll have some coffee before you leave, Renart had said, ouais?

Ana didn't want to trouble him, he had work to do, she was sure, but it was really no trouble, bad form not to offer, bad form to refuse indeed, and in truth, Erehwynan etiquette aside, a conversation that did not careen from what Jaq smelled between his toes to how he would have slept in ancient Gaul, to where he'd heard of vintage doublets going cheap, to when the fob was at its brightest in the sky, to why pirates could be deemed utopian anarchists, to whether gravity had changed the taste of meat on Mars, to which poor farmyard fowl the hero of Gargantua by François Rabelais concluded and maintained to be without comparison as an arsewipe... really, Renart had said, some mature discourse for a change would be a mercy.

So they sit at the kitchen table, sipping espresso poured from a stainless steel macchinetta into equally Neo-Modern glazed red clay ochoko, chatting about Ana's phantoms, pataphysician and pataphysicist fumbling for a common language.

Corbin, says Renart. I *think* I savvy where you are with Corbin, but it still seems... sneakily mystical. How are you *not* saying that these phantoms exist on some aetherial plane—higher, deeper, orthogonal, whatever?

That's *exactly* what I'm not saying: alethic persistence is not epistemic continuity; span is not stint on another level, running on another track in the same direction. Look, Corbin is a good start point, but...

Corbin is pataphysics's alchemy, she's trying to express, a corm that has to be devoured for the actual science to sprout. From alchemy to chemistry, and onward. And now, here, ages down the line, they're flowers on an ancient tree, physician and physicist. Talking of transmutation of elements from here and now doesn't mean turning lead into gold. But it sounds a whole lot like it, Renart reckons. Sounds like her hylenet phantoms are nothing less than gods in the wind.

A god, singular, uncapitalised. There's only been one agency gleaned in that medium so far, Ana tells him.

•

THE OLD XANTHEAN couple nod friendly smiles and dints of intro as they pass, hand in hand, Asa and Nkoyo Edet, who are, the politely backdinting Jaq Cartier—*with Puk Massinger, intro per pro*—gleans from a glance to profile, in Erehwyna to celebrate their twenty-fifth wedding anniversary. Which is barely in Jaq's nous before Puk, slick off the mark, bounces a felicitation via him that turns both women's smiles to the beaming warmth, now over the shoulder and with crinkling eyes, of aged aunts charmed by a posy gifted *quite out of the blue* by some young niece's chivalric paramour. Being Xantheans, their gratitude is as sincere as it's effusive—*Why, thank you both so much!*—and echoed in a fuss of warmth, an old dear's whisper as Mesdames Edet amble for the steps up to the folly: What *lovely* young men.

Debonair, says Jaq with a prod of elbow in Puk's side. If you can't hack the Erehwynan swagger, least you can always move to Xanthe.

Oh, I can hack the swagger, says Puk. Earlier was just a side-swipe. I wasn't ready.

And now you are?

If this Libertine Meadow's as wild as you paint, I'm not *that* bashful; ask Ana. It's just... high kicks in the chorus line versus spotlight out of nowhere and *dance, monkey, dance!*

A hint of pout. Jaq drapes an arm around Puk's shoulder as they take the path for the Arboretum doors.

In that case, he says, I was fancying we might cast it on my tumblespace. That'd be peachy, ouais?

Willpower alone keeps him blithe and eyes front, playing fox with startled bunny, poised through the pause.

Sure, says Puk with trembling bravado. Sure, why not?

Jaq squeezes him in a headlock hug and loosens, scrumples Puk's hair.

Soothe, he says, just joshing. Truth is, I've got a niftier scheme, sudden notion. Come on.

He stretches his free arm out as they pass the date-plum tree planted just inside the doors, bouncing fingers like a nipper rattling a stick along railings, riffling leaf just for the relish of the moment.

•

SHE IS DECIDUOUS, *Diospyros lotus,* a tree of glossy, glabrous leaves of an ovate form and leathery feel, five to fifteen centimetres long, three to six centimetres wide, shed in winter. Her aging bark she sheds as she grows, striving for a height of fifteen to thirty metres in optimum conditions, generally falling short. She was once the daughter of the Titan Nereus. Lotis was her name. She lived in a world of feasts, a party girl, fell asleep in a drunken blur once, was woken by the braying of the satyr Silenus's ass; that was the crowd she hung out with. She would have fitted in well in Erehwyna, frolic-fucking on Libertine Meadow, casting on tumblespace.

She is dioecious. Her flowers are small and yellowy-green, unassuming, which seems at odds with the tale of Dryope being taken with her bloom, unless perhaps, after the plucking that doomed poor Dryope, Lotis reconsidered her own gaudiness, settled on a less alluring perianth. Regardless, these flowers appear in June or July, bearing seeds with thin skin and a hard endosperm, fruit ripening from October to November. It might have been a festival at the turn of autumn to winter when the braying ass woke her, come to think of it. Whatever. She woke to find Priapus leering over her, his ithyphallus like the club of Herakles—albeit wilting at the raucous hee-haw and her wakening. She shoved him away and ran.

She is delicious. The small fruit, only a few centimetres in diameter, ambercream in colour, not as vibrant orange as a pumpkin or persimmon, but approaching it, is harsh and astringent until fully ripe. If left to cool however, to be frosted, to rot a little even, then this bletting brings out the rich flavour in her juicy flesh, the blend of plummy and dateish (more notable when dried) that gives the fruit its common name—date-plum. The botanical designation of the genus meanwhile comes from her name in ancient Greece, *dios pyros,* meaning *wheat of Zeus* or *fruit of gods,* suggesting no small appreciation.

Priapus went beyond appreciation to would-be rapist prick, chased her until her patience broke. If he ever got the message that she'd rather be a tree than be fucked by him, she doesn't know; the word *no* is too subtle for some, it seems, for those dicks to whom *drunk* equals *asking for it* and rejection indicates the null hanker of frigidity or the sixer kinsey of a lesbian.

She sighs as Susurrus slips in the opening doors just to kiss hello, slips back out as they close, following the fleshlings who, contrary to the arrant cock-fluffery of your all too common Priapus, she would totally do if she were still that party girl. They seem quite sweet even barely ripened.

She is dense and dark in the secondary xylum of her trunk. Of the woods known as ebony, many have been of her genus—which would seem apt for the lotus trees under the shade of which, so we are told in the Book of Job, Behemoth lies, in a covert of reeds and marsh, surrounded by the willows of the brook.

IV

•

Puk, with the assistance of one locker room bench of red-painted wood on basalt blocks, undresses.

Jerkin: synthe filigree three-quarter length jacket, fitted to the waist, flared below; fabric charcoal, thread silvery, pattern paisley; already unbuttoned, now slipped off and hung on peg in locker. *Boots:* black leather balmorals, polished; knots on both untied first; left lace loosened and boot levered off; ditto right boot; picked up together with one hand; stowed neatly at the back of the locker, toes facing out. *Socks:* charcoal grey cotton, non-odiferous; removed individually; laid flat on bench with heel underneath, one atop the other; rolled tight from the toes; aperture of bottom sock stretched round and over to capsule neatly; stowed in right boot. *Trews:* drainpipes of same fabric and style as jerkin; unbuttoned and slid down to thighs; left leg then right hauled off from seated wobble on bench; flapped and folded once vertically, bringing legs together, then twice horizontally; package deposited in locker frontwise of boots. *Jersey:* stretch cotton, skin-nipped, silver with charcoal grey raglan sleeves; peeled off from waist; turned right side out; folded twice vertically, bringing sleeves together, then over body; folded horizontally letter-style, top-third down then over again; stowed on top of trews. *Skivvies:* stretch cotton hip-cut trunks, charcoal grey; peeled off with thumbs and flapped; folded once vertically and stowed on top of jersey.

He picks up the towel from the bench, unfurls and drapes it over his arm. Finds himself the object of Jaq's twinkly eye.

Jaq—who's just chucked his doublet on the bench, yanked the drawstring to his britches loose to let them drop, and stepped awkwardly out to balance with arms, prise off his plimsolls with his toes—stands naked, cradling his scooped up togs. He shoves them in his locker, smiling schtum.

Margaritifer Pilsener on top, a couple popped out of the clutch, one each for now—It's not an Erehwynan sauna without beer, he says—then it's lockers closed and they're ready. Jaq picks up his own towel, flips it over his shoulder.

This way.

•

A SHRUB OR small tree of yellowish-white wood called *Commiphora myrrha* grows her thick trunk to around five metres tall cursed by Aphrodite for scorning her suitors to fall in lust with her father Cinyras of Cyprus back when her name was Myrrha from a Semitic root meaning *bitter* because she was so wrought and despairing to the point of suicide her trunk swollen to store water as succulent as she is short to suffer drought for long stints of her nine months trudge through the palms of swelteringArabia the fields of Panchaea and all because her nurse halted her hanging and hairless throughout with flaky bark of silvery blue-grey whitish or ruddy hue peeling papery to a photosynthetic green underbark Myrrha coerced the woman with threats of successful suicide to help her consummate incestuous desire during the Festival of Ceres when no women were to be touched by men for nine days as she produces numerous knotted spiny branches and orthogonal branchlets stiff and spreading each ending in a spine as sharp as her father's sword she fled from all the way to Sabaea with him hot on her heels on her twigs sparse single leaves small and even minute at times on petioles short or long from a millimetre to a centimetre arranged irregular or alternate often tri-foliolate pinnately compound with two tiny leaflets at the base of the main where the nurse found Cinyras drunk in his bed and offered a maiden keen to step in for his wife a girl of Myrrha's age she said when he asked of leaves grey-green and chartaceous with three or four weak main veins slightly tooth-letted at the apex lateral smooth as the touch of her sneaking into his bed in utter darkness for a fistful of nights maybe six to forty millimetres long and three to twenty millimetres wide and as variable in shape as in size maybe spathulate lanceolate or elliptic maybe attenuate cuneate rounded or truncate at the base maybe apically rounded or acute as the desire to know her identity that led Cinyras to light a lamp one night to find that in autumn the leaves turn yellow before they fall to their knees in Sabaea where the gods took pity on her clustered panicles of tiny inconspicuous flowers dioecious with male flowers usually precocious three to four millimetres long and on a very short stalk a four-toothed calyx at its base her smooth brown ovate fruit two to four millimetres long she wept on her knees an aromatic oleoresin yellowish clear or opaque from bark that was split once after her metamorphosis to deliver Adonis sweet as her sap used with natron by the Egyptians in embalming used as medicine or perfume or incense used in the Ketoret during the time of the Tabernacle and the First and Second Temple periods offered on the altar of incense and brought by the Magi as a gift for the infant Yeshua

•

After the cool slip-slap of wet soles on white tile as they padded through, shaking limbs still drippling fresh from the showers, the pool room's chlorine scent and rippled blue light, the sauna is a crib that snuggles them to the warmth of its welcome, a crib in clean-edged cedar cladding and air soft with the aroma of malted grain, tinged with camphor and forests. Incense in a Nordic church of steam, its altar the stove, its few worshippers sat on the half dozen tiers of bench that line the starboard and larboard walls: a couple of old men on the top right tier, in the corner closest to the door; to the left, a family sat two up, two down on middle tiers; a group of three women back left, top tier.

No intros in the sauna, just polite nods.

Jaq twists his Margaritifer open as he ushers Puk in, pulls the door shut sharpish. He takes a slug and guides the Earther to a seat across from the family, spreads his towel. Puk lays his own towel down beside and sets to sit, halts to dither unsure when Jaq instead heads to the back of the room, beckons a follow-me to the stove, where the Erehwhynan drips the tiniest splash on the coals. Nods for Puk to follow suit.

Not too much, says Jaq. It's just—that's it—just custom.

Jaq's sizzle and Puk's hiss thicken the scent ever so slightly, malted barley and hops.

It smells like baking bread, whispers Puk as they take their seats. Nifty.

He sips his beer, inhales the wavelet of perfumed heat. Jaq leans back to bask; already the warmth is kneading flesh, steeping bone.

Time stretches, shift softening in the quietude to glide its stint. From tick to tick. To slickening of skin. To trickle of beaded sweat. Down back.

Sometimes *dull* and *blunt* are the wrong terms for low shift; this is one of those times.

Löyly? says one of the women after a while not measured in minutes, palm proffering the wooden water bucket and ladle down by the stove.

With a look to Jaq for his lead, Puk adds his nod to everyone else's, watches the woman clamber down. She dips the ladle, picks up a jug sat on the lowest bench and drips a little liquid onto the water before pouring it on the coals. Oil of Erehwyna. Its extracts and essences waft on the wave of heat that comes now, softly fierce, brutally cozy. Musks and resins in a wash of breathtaking ardour. Myrrh. Frankincense.

•

BROUGHT BY THE Magi as a gift for the infant Yeshua and used in the Ketoret during the time of the Tabernacle and the First and Second Temple periods offered on the altar of incense she is the incense of all incenses in her name even frankincense made from her pale yellow resin with the slightest greenish tint stickier than gum but may be chewed like such in Ayurvedic medicine to treat arthritis heal wounds strengthen women's hormone systems and purify the air of germs by burning to cleanse one's house with her psychoactive smoke every day for good health and relief of depression her aroma symbolising life itself her resin blended with oils in Judaic Christian and Islamic faiths to anoint newborns and novices to a new spiritual phase loved by the sun god Helios she was known as Persian princess Leukothoe buried in sand by her father when he learned of the affair oh but her lover transformed her to the tree *Boswellia sacra* with her compound leaves and odd number of leaflets covered with a fine down when first sprouted and growing opposite one another along branches bearing her tiny yellowish white flowers gathered in axillary clusters composed of five petals ten stamens and a cup with five teeth afterward bearing a fruit which is a capsule of about one centimetre long but most of all bearing this milky ichor that coagulates in contact with air and can be charred and ground into kohl by the Egyptians for black eyeliner produced when the small deciduous tree reaches eight to ten years old and a height of two to eight metres with one or more trunks with a bulbous disk-like swelling at the base that will anchor her during the most savage storms so she may grow not just in rocky soil or gravel but in desolate regions directly out of solid rock as a hardy survivor whose tears with their more fragrant aroma are considered superior extracted via a small shallow cut on her trunk or branch or by easily removing a section of her bark with the texture of paper to drain this resin for collection by hand the tapping done two or three times a year with the highest quantities of aromatic terpene and diterpen and sesquiterpene to be found in those most precious tears of the final tap

•

A STRETCH OF slow relish, supine on the top tier, Jaq pillows his head in fingerlaced hands, crooks one leg up, slips the other long, toes pointed. Puk smoothes his towel on the bench below and settles, skims sweat from his arm with a slick of hand, a flick. Slippage coheres to ticklish beads all over his body, rivulets down the small of his back, his flanks; a runnel from jugular notch down sternum halts to regather before trickling down to navel. The whole experience is as sensual as the Sybarite's rose petal bed that Johnson detailed in his dictionary, yet simple as Spartan living, Scandinavian light. He glances over his shoulder at Jaq's laze, the naked form graced to nude. And not remotely lewd, to be honest.

Even with the sauna to themselves now, Puk savvies why Jaq said, on the way, that hanker wouldn't enter into it, no matter if the place was crammed shoulder to shoulder with Erehwyna's buffest braves, sat thigh to thigh, along each bench, on every bench, flesh pressing flesh, even so's Puk was sat with Jaq's knees spread to pincer his shoulders and some stud below betwixt his own. Heat high enough to scald if it wasn't too hot for steam to condense, don't be gulled, Jaq said, by Tempe casters orgying in their bathhouse brothels over tumblespace. Those aren't *real* saunas, not *Erehwynan* saunas. Sure, every Erehwynan kidster, lass or lad, at some point *fancies* to fuck in the steam; they glean sharpish it's more slog than jape.

True enough, the heat saps all yen to languid abstraction. Puk ekes the last drips of his pilsener, sits the empty down at his side.

He hadn't expected debauchery, to be fair, but he did daydream the flirtations of ancient Athenian baths, athletes oiled from the gymnasia and palaestrae, sprucing for symposia. He fancied latter-day ephebes scrubbing down with cleansing sands, splashing hot water over their bodies, showering under the maws of marble lions, flicking water at each other. Exiting dark vaulted steam baths for a cooling plunge, for a lounge on the tiered steps of circular pools, for a massage with aromatic oils. That is, as the interworld tells him, as he blathered to Jaq last night in the tabac on Boulevard Hovendaal where they met a carousal of Jaq's cadres for tabac and beer, how homo hankers gleaned their potentials in those days, dinting with glances.

Or in the annual kissing contest at the tomb of Diocles, he said, where all the boychiks vied to see whose smooch was superior.

Shim had dumped beer glasses full to jauping on the table then, betwixt them, noogied Jaq's head and whispered sly in his ear, dodged his shove away with a laugh. Volutes of smoke caught the low light in their crowded booth. Jaq looked back at him, his gold eyes keen. You were saying?

Athens, said Puk. They savvied how to do courtship in Athens. A suitor would sleep all night on the steps of his beloved's house, just to show his commitment. Nifty, huh?

Jaq leaned over to sip his beer without lifting, shrugged.

I'd do that, he said.

He looked up, backhand wiping a dribble from his chin, and the moment spun, unfolding to a sky.

It still is, in the snug now of the sauna, is still unfolding as Puk leans back, stretches his arms along the bench above, to soak.

I've been thinking, says Jaq.

He turns his head, his fire opal eyes.

And? says Puk.

•

AND... I GIVE up, says Ana. You're impossible.

I'll spot you the trust, says Renart. That you know what you're talking about. But I'm afraid I just can't see sentience *without* shift.

Fair enough, she concedes. Most people can't.

She lifts the ochoko to sip, but finds it long since empty of all but coffee silt, sets it back down on the table by the vase of hyacinths from the other night, the walnut bowl replenished with apples. Shrouded bread on a board. A scramble of coins. The mirror is hung above now, a rack of a dozen wine flasks in its place, where the table nestles the back wall of the room. Perched on her stool, back to the armchairs of evening, Ana twiddles a stray honey dipper as Renart, toddling in the kitchen area, dumps the macchinetta on the stove, rummages jars on the counter, cabinets above. Returns with bowls and jars—which jogs a call for the hour, a dint in her nous.

Shitsack! she says. I didn't realise. I should go.

He's already back at the counter, bringing a breadknife in one hand, a jar in the other.

Except, she says, you're about to tell me that would be a heinous insult, right?

He laughs and lays the knife on the table, twists the cork from the jar.

Actually, it would be rude of me to hold you now. That said, if you're feeling at all peckish...

•

SHE IS A small drab drupe in Ana's hand, one to two and half centimetres in diameter, grey-green, picked last season from an orchard cultivar of Harmakhis and so fleshier than the fruit of her wilder selves. Within her flesh is a pit, within the pit a span of shifts to come, an evergreen tree or shrub, short and squat, her gnarled trunk seldom over eight to fifteen metres tall, her leaves arranged opposite and decussate, narrow and lanceolate, four to ten centimetres long, one to three centimetres wide, silvery-green, racemose panicles springing from their axils, the flowers small and white, fragrant and feathery, with four sepals and petals, two stamens and bifid stigma. Within the tree is her ancient history, shift of the past, her name as a maiden dear to Athena, Moria.

When Athena and Poseidon bickered for dominion of Athens, it was her death that won the contest set by Zeus, the city staked as prize for the deity who produced the greatest gift for humans. While the god of the sea conjured the horse from wash of waves, wise and flashing-eyed Athena transformed her dying Moria to the sacred *Olea europaea*, planted her in the rock of the Acropolis, in her sanctuary. She was to become the most important tree of the whole region's horticulture. Her leaves crowned victors at the Olympics. Her oil was used for skin and hair, for lamps to light the night, for cooking. With just a little balsamic vinegar, as Renart drizzles now into the bowl where she is also, she can make fresh bread transcend its own perfection.

In the Linear B syllabic script of Mycenaea, she had another name, e-ra-wa or elaiva, from which is derived her more common monicker: olive.

•

JAQ SETS THE Harmakhis olives down on the treehouse floor, unruckles an edge of the quilt for the bread and cheese, which he lays down, unwraps. Then the wine, which he wedges betwixt crossed legs and groin while he twists the corkscrew in, latches and levers it to a happy pop. Then slumps shoulders in sudden realisation, bites back the fricative of a *fuckwit*.

I forgot the cups, he mumbles.

Puk, with Apple Mouse in one hand nibbling at apple core in the other, shrugs.

We can glug from the flask, like barbarians. It'll add savour: lashings of blackcurrant, butter, bitumen, and the slightest hint of Jaq slobber.

Delicious. Hang on, I have a fancy.

Jaq fences a private corral in his own interworld domain, dints Puk the entry, and gets the backdint in his nous as Puk slips in.

A private cast? says Puk. Sordid, I hope.

Husht, says Jaq. I need to concentrate.

He holds his hand up in a shallow scoop, as a beggar staring at the insult of a button for alms. Snapshots so the image, cut off at the wrist, hangs in the air as he drops his hand and calls a lathe method; the curve of hand rotated three hundred and sixty degrees blends into a bowl: a rim of fingertips hooped with keratin of fingernails; inside, the negative space shaped by a palm's turning through time. Ridges of interphalangeal joints and metacarpophalangeal knuckles run round the exterior, but Jaq smoothes these with a focused shift of stancer skill—he could carve a perfect circle with his toe, blindfolded. A few more strokes of shift and the simwork might be some Tibetan singing bowl of carnelian flesh.

Nifty, says Puk. I'm not clicking how we drink with it though.

Husht.

Jaq gleans an image of yellow-fruited ivy from a botany interface, patinas the keratin hoop with it. Flicks the whole aside to call from a personal library: Ana snapped candid on the night of her first visit in a smiling glance, head turning to a comment, one eyebrow raised. He raids a stock of Renart to construct a rivalry of two suitors, render her shift of gaze a look from this to that. A little dress-up interface for kidsters and he has two peplos-clad Renarts vying to serenade Puk's sister, one with lyre, the other with pipes. He capsules the tableaux, stows it larboard. A snapshot of himself stood on the basalt rock below, aged to infirmity, accoutred with net, becomes an old fisherman—also capsuled, also stowed. One of Puk sat in the sauna—

Hey, when did you... ?

I'm *always* recording.

—becomes a kidster perched on a drystone wall, guarding a vineyard, fiddling asphodels into a weavework cage for crickets. Two sleekit foxes nail this tableaux—a tod skulking the vines, a vixen pitting her wits against the kidster's satchel, unnoticed. Jaq plucks the bowl back into play, sets it turning as he sizes and styles each scene, skims the view he wants, applies it to the vessel. When he's done, afloat in the air betwixt Martian and Earther, the bowl is not perhaps a *faithful* facsimile of a black-figure kalyx but it's true in spirit.

Straight out of Theocritus, says Puk.

Sod all use for drinking, say Jaq, but it's the thought that counts, ouais?

By the end of their stint in the andreion of the treehouse, if they're to cleave to the archaic protocols of the kidnapping, Jaq should have given his kleinos: a drinking cup; military attire; an ox. The last may require a dunt and shoogle into the symbolic, a nudge of leeway, but here and now he can and does conjure this first shift of friendship, romance even, to something beyond. He capsules the simulacrum and sends it, collapses the corral, then it's just the two of them in the treehouse, sat crosslegged face-to-face. Just them and Apple, who Puk sets down in the nest of his togs as Jaq passes him the flask of Kasei red.

To the summer, says Jaq.

To all of them, says Puk.

•

DID HE SAY *summer* or *Sumer?* Ampelos breathes out of the flask to ask.

Summer, says Susurrus.

Simmer? says Ampelos. *Shimmer?*

Summer, says Susurrus. And you heard just fine.

Ampelos snickers and drifts in the godling's embrace, twirls a little wisp of scent to tickle Puk's nose.

You don't remember Sumer, do you? he says to the wind. I remember Sumer. It *was* very summery, simmery—shimmery too. I was there.

At home in humid forests and at the sides of streams, Mesopotamia wasn't an ideal climate for him, but he was known, the grape vine, *Vitis vinifera*, a liana with flaky bark and a sap used in Medieval Europe as ointment for infections of skin and eye. Growing to thirty five metres high, his leaves, arranged alternate, palmately lobed, five to twenty centimetres long and broad, were used to wrap delectable dolma—though that was later, really, more Arabia than Sumer, and—

And in America, says Susurrus, those leaves were mulched to a poultice for haemorrhoids. Does that count as homeopathy? A pain in the arse treated with a pain in the arse?

Ampelos blows a raspberry, doesn't care. He *was* there, in the cradle of civilisation. Read the Epic of Gilgamesh if you don't believe it: oldest story of the fleshlings' scrivings, and there he is, being poured out by a barmaid called Siduri in a tavern at the end of the world. He always tickled to that tale, saw a seed of himself in furry Enkidu, wild child of the watering hole who tamed a wanton king.

Haemorrhoids, he mumps. It was his grapes the mortals made most use of anyways: unripe for coughs and catarrh; ripe for cancer and cholera; dried to raisins, steeped and puréed, as a tonic for consumption; soured to retorts, spat in spite, as a sauce for petty quarrels. And squished and fermented to wine, of course, above all else, to be tasted in toasts down through the aeons, from a tavern in the neolithic mythscape to this treehouse here on Mars.

Puk raises the flask to his lips, and Ampelos tingles to the kiss, transformed in the touch of a tongue to pepper and vanilla, cloves and smoke.

He was a youth of Thrace once, Ampelos, son of satyr and nymph, beloved of Dionysos. Horned little devil, a beardless boy but hairy-legged and hoofed as Pan, he played Tarzan, d'Artagnan, Alexander on Bucephalus, swinging down from an elm tree to land astraddle a wild bull, to ride it, whooping boasts to the moon cow, Selene: Look at me! Look at me! Her spite sent the sting of a gadfly, and Ampelos was thrown and trampled. Which sucked, needless to say. Being trampled by Dionysus after the metamorphosis, the deity's pink toes all wriggling in Ampelos's juices as he taught humans the arts of viticulture and vinification—that wasn't so bad. Toes are at least sexy, Ampelos reckons. Hoofs not so much.

Jaq kisses him now, and he's chilli and sarsaparilla, cinnamon and oak—another self on another palate... but then, who isn't? He lingers a little on the fleshling's lips, starts a stain that will be there even after the flask is done, there to mingle sarsaparilla and vanilla in the mash of lovers' lips. He'll be gone before it gets too steamy he suspects, the last drip licked from the flask's lip, bouquet stolen away by his own breezy beau, but so it goes, and it's a sweet goodbye to dissolve into the savour of flesh, of skin and salt. Besides, he'll only be gone from here, elsewhere his fruits even now ripening towards purply-black with a pale wax bloom, small in his wild species, only six millimetres in diameter or so, much larger in his cultivated species—of the vineyards of Kasei, say—up to three centimetres long, and as often green or red.

Puk takes the proffered flask back, raises it in another toast: To us.

This is my blood of the covenant, a would-be godling of love once said, and generations after fancied that the wine, he meant, had transubstantiated to his holy ichor. Ampelos knows it was the other way around, that Yeshua's blood became, in that moment, wine, the sacrament a libation sipped through his sad smiling lips, a tipple of sensual pleasure swigged and offered round to sanctify the flesh that had forgotten its divinity. Remember, he was saying, and let every taste be a communion with the holy world of vines and veins, of loaves and lives. And all the follies of his followers were sown in the misunderstanding of that moment.

To us, says Jaq.

•

JAQ, PRIMPING IN the mirror, admiring a shiner got from an arsewipe's fist. Jaq, in Renart's study before the interview, fingers raised to trace with wonder the laurel wreath awarded to this maestro he so yearns to prentice to. Jaq, slugging back a cup of red wine and rising, in a tabac on Boulevard Hovendaal, to shove an ageling who sneered at *stunted dirter* Puk. Jaq, lazing on the sofa, gazing off into tumblespace as he waits for bread to bake, relishing the aroma. Jaq, sat at the kitchen table, counting coins to glean if he can afford the vintage doublet yet. Jaq, dribbling honey into Puk's mouth from the dipper, trickling it in rogueish glee over lips and cheeks, nose and neck, as the Earther flaps *enough! enough!* Jaq, fumbling a Devonshire Quarrenden out of his satchel, offering it to Puk in outstretched hand, in the treehouse.

Renart sets the stances of Jaq into a Solomon's Seal down in the courtyard, a framework for his abstractions: magnanimity; esteem; courage; poise; prudence; gusto; ardour. The last sits at the centre.

In the Holy Roman Empire, they sermonised of seven cardinal vices, seven virtues born in the scorn of sin: humility in scorn of pride; kindness in scorn of envy; patience in scorn of wrath; diligence in scorn of sloth; generosity in scorn of greed; temperance in scorn of gluttony; chastity in scorn of lust. Aristotle, with his navigable mean, would say we have only half the story here; we must imagine the starboard shoals if we run too far from sinister larboard, overcorrect in terror of temptation. We must imagine: humility become *shame*, and kindness *condescension*; patience become *timidity*, and diligence *zeal*; charity become *unction*, and temperance *austerity*; chastity become *mortification*.

Alexander's tutor might not have called these virtues and vices *stance*, but he savvied more than any fool Platonist or Pythagorean that it's all a matter of attitude in action, whether it be to one's own achievement or another's, to conflict or impetus, reserve or expense, or appetence. And this is the base of the stance Renart seeks to articulate, which is itself a stance to a stance, a response to the Romans, past, present and future—because if the Geisters carry that scorn of sin into their secular faith, Renart rather doubts it will ever disappear. There is no utopia, not here and now, not ever.

Still, if the Good Christian is set against the Wicked Heathen, whether named as such or not, the Good Heathen may be set against the Wicked Christian, scorning the hamartia from shame to mortification for their antitheses...

Magnanimity, esteem, courage, poise, prudence, gusto, ardour.

And the greatest of these is ardour.

•

WE'VE DECIDED TO become Greeks, says Jaq, erastes and eromenos.

Or philetor and kleinos, says Puk, if we go ancient Cretan.

You're sure it's not *cretin?* says Ana. Do I really want to know what this is about?

Jak twiddled his kinsey to a sixer, says Puk. Just for me.

And my hanker, says Jak, all the way up! We're synched as Xantheans now.

Homo sapiens sapiens homo, says Puk, both of us through and through.

It's a proud tradition, says Jaq. Heroic.

Pausanius, says Puk, in the Republic, says the bond of erastes and eromenos is stronger than any despot's thrall.

Phaedrus, says Jaq, in the Symposium, says with an army made of lovers fighting at each other's side, even a handful could take on the world.

Plato, says Ana, putting words in their mouths. And to dispute them, as I recall.

Plutarch, says Puk, points to the Sacred Band of Thebes. Tempers the manner and character of the youth, he says.

Hieronymus, says Jaq, claims it was all the rage because such pairings had brought down tyrants in their prime.

Chariton and Melanippus!

Harmodius and Aristogeiton!

Theognis of Megara, proclaims Puk: *Happy is the lover who works out naked, and then goes home to sleep all day with a beautiful boy.* His beautiful boy going by the name of Kyrnos.

Mine going by the name of Puk. If it's OK with you?

You're asking my permission? says Ana.

For the harpagmos, says Jaq. The abduction.

•

An Erehwynan greeting: left hand on shoulder, right hand on hip; kiss on the left cheek, kiss on the right. This the fourth in immediate sequence for Puk, and wholly extraneous, a consequence of being dropped from Ana's skimpod outside Maman and Papa Cartier's townhouse to knock nervy, be answered with doggy lavishings of Jaq's attention, whirled in through two previous such salutations with the Cartier parentals and more rousy ramstouger ranniganting hello hello hellos on the floor with old Diogenes who clearly didn't believe in age at all, and who was clearly a core influence in Jaq's stancings of welcome, or perhaps vice versa, and then with barely an *It was nice to finally meet you* huchled out and down along flagstoned streets busy with skimpods, skirting the Old Town, to the summer-crowded esplanade, to the docks specifically where Jaq first clocked and queried the newly-sprung Earther, in honour of their three week and two day anniversary, to meet the mates for *something*, Jaq slyly evaded, *special*, and there they were, Joi, Shim and Don, so it was Erehwynan greetings again all round, three for Jaq and three for Puq, formal with Joi, friendly with Don, frolicsome with Shim who smackered his cheeks and slipped hand up from hip to kittle his ribs, whispering she was so glad for Jaq's lucky score, fluttering Puk so that afore he even knew it he was turning arms out to greet Jaq too, doh, but Jaq just shrugged and laughed and drew him into a superfluous embrace, because why not?

And now Puk, thinking of kissing contests at the tomb of Diocles, catches Jaq's arms before he breaks the embrace, gets a quizzical face in return. He slides the wrist of the hand on his shoulder up, to his neck, to a caress of cheek, of jaw, that becomes a tuck of chin, a search for meaning: *what are you up to?* He peels Jaq's other hand from his hip and brings it—Jaq glances down, then back to his gaze, with a bat of blinkers—round to the front, sets it to cup his tackle, which he feels scrinch itself in anticipation.

It is a scene from classical terracotta, Athenian ochre enacted in flesh, one of three set postures that were used to paint the course of a relationship. It is the courtship of erastes and eromenos; the erastes stands, one hand fondling the youth's genitals, the other cradling chin to look him in the eye.

Except Jaq's gaze slips away and past him now, over Puk's shoulder.

Now, says he.

V

•

Really? he says.

Renart strumps about from room to room, mumping and mulligrumphing, thrunched by the right moger of the place to a crunkle of brow and a clamp on the jut of his chaft, thumb under chin, forefinger curling up under pursed lips. Over the weeks of merry visits from Ana, it seemed, primarily to gab in billows of blue smoke over red wine and only secondarily to salve her sisterly fret that Puk—ensconced in the treehouse with Jaq but making regular barbarian raids on civilisation for the sake of grub or ablution—was *not hassling Renart to distraction, I hope,* curious prodding finally won from her, yesterday evening, an admission that all Renart's return jaunts into Erehwyna have indeed been diverted to work, café, park, restaurant, tavern, tabac, in short any elsewhere than the Massinger home, because in all the stint they've been here she still hasn't sorted it to presentable.

Presentable? Renart says, having coaxed acceptance of a pataphysician's eye and hand, it being, after all, his art to hone a life's ergonomics to healthy set of attitude, flesh and environs. Presentable? he says, having followed dinted directions, turned down into the culvert off Rue Stroedeker and arrived on the doorstep at the crack of noon, to stroll in, smiling assurances—*It can't be that bad*—and scope the full horror of misplaced furniture and furnishings, boxes and crates, cases and contents that he might describe as half-stacked and half-strewn were it not for the implication of balance in those halves. Ana, how is this even *habitable?*

He weaves the chaos, room to room, wireframing the small ground floor apartment, square hall with pisser and scrubber on the left on entry, back suite and study beside, kitchen-cum-salon and master suite to the right, looking out on Stroedeker and sunshine. Cosy but ceilinged high, with fine pine parquet underfoot throughout. Light grey though, on the walls, a bachelor's fashion of two decades ago, grim style of some strutter stancing dull machismo which, Ana explains, she didn't have the tick to update. And as for the rest... she just didn't glean a *start* for it.

He studies her for a tick, and the clutter of her attributes around.

Not a shock, he says. There is no start from here.

It's not her, he means, the shade, so implacably not her that she's surely sensed the futility of trying to crunk her life into this drabness; but so blandly shamming functionality that, like as not, it sold her on a lie of being passable, an unassuming blankness offering itself as plain backdrop for anyone and everyone: one shade fits all. As if everyone and anyone worked like that.

What you have here, he says, is a quiddity trap.

Quiddity, the whatness of an object, is the *essential*, the nature of a thing as an instance of its class. Haccaeity, the thisness of an object, is the *existential*, the nature of a thing as construct of quirks defying reduction to quiddity. In the era of Davenport, the deluge of machined objects made for an angst of drowning. Without the notion of projectivity, where was the haccaeity of factoried chow and togs, flatpack fittings and gimcrack commodities? Where even the thisness in a pleasure become parlance, formulated for replication as geekware loaded in the meat machines? In the Society of the Spectacle, as she herself has lived the fallout of, post-modernity, post-singularity, even a human seemed all quiddity, quirks merely the unique settings of shared attributes. Skinsacks with a tuple of signifiers inside that could be scanned into a simulacrum—geist as soul, Ana would say, for those who scorned superstition but could not surrender it.

Davenport broached a new paradigm in abolition of quiddity, his supposition: that in every corral of objects abstractable to a class by common attributes and behaviours, every object in that corral is not merely distinct in its unique mix of attribute settings but cannot be fully described without recourse to attributes inapplicable to all others of its class.

Not only is *this* electron not equal to *that* electron, but it is not equivalent.

This, Renart says, is a shade for everyone and therefore no one.

So. Arms folded, Renart stands in the master bedsuite, brooding on a wall, glancing now and then at Ana, at the scatterings of jumble. The haccaeity of this canny scientist sprawling out around her in a humidor of Kaseians on the mantlepiece, a sim syrinx propped upright in a corner, the sleeves cut off her Geister jerkin, actually, he thinks, this shouldn't be so gnarly. He's rather savvy of Ana's haccaeity by now, and fond of it.

•

RESOUNDING THE CLOMP of fleshling feet and shifting furniture upon her patchwork panels, bouncing back their voices in the emptying room she floors, Pitys can't help but think back fondly on the old days of Arcadia, of mountain heights, ravines, and shepherds calling out to hear their echoes in the hills she cloaked as the pine tree, *Pinus pinea,* or sturdier still in her Stone Pine form, and tall and proud, growing some twelve to twenty metres high, and even over twenty-five sometimes.

The shifts of life, she thinks. She's sure of all her kind she senses shift most keenly. Senses? *Undergoes* more like. She *lives* shift, not as sharply as the fleshlings tromping in and out the master bedsuite of the Massinger abode, shuffling with weights between them, dropping a clatter or thump of something now and then, and cursing or being cursed for it—*Rot and bones, Puk! Give that here!*—no, not *that* sharply, but more keen than many a tree. She displays it as she grows.

In youth? Ah, in youth she is a bushy globe and, for her first five to ten years, bears leaves that mark her juvenile, growing as little singletons, blue-green and glaucous, a mere snip of two to four centimetres long, quite different from the adult leaves that start to sprout amidst these from the fourth or fifth year on, five times the length—sometimes as much as thirty centimetres long, indeed, albeit those are quite exceptional—mid-green and growing bundled into twos. By her tenth year, roughly speaking, though she might still sprout some juvenile leaves in regrowth after injury, a broken shoot or whatnot, just to show that she still can, those mature leaves have usurped the juvenile entirely, and she'll spread a wide umbrella canopy from her thick trunk with its thick bark, red-brown, carved by deep fissures into broad vertical plates. In full maturity she sports a broad and flat crown forty to sixty metres wide.

She doesn't rush all shifts, of course. It takes three years, a longer stint than any other pine requires, for her broad ovoid cones to reach maturity at eight to fifteen centimetres long. Within these cones, pine nuts or piñones, pinhões or pinoli, her seeds are large, two centimetres long, pale brown beneath the powdery black coat that rubs off to a gentle thumb. The crude four to eight millimetre wing on each is like to fall off on its own, but then it's largely ineffective for dispersal by Susurrus anyway, so her seeds are animal-dispersed—mainly by the azure-winged magpie once upon a time, but these days mostly by the fleshlings who, it seems, find her a useful wood for furniture or floors. Like the floor of this townhouse apartment, which is bare now, bedsuite hollowed by the fleshlings, one of whom crouches to stroke her, bless him, calls a question that soon gets its answer in a fumbling of armfuls in through the doorway, followed shortly by grand flappings that spread out the dustsheets, lay them softly down now, to protect her.

It's not the reverence of antiquity, but she can't help but be reminded of it. On Mount Mainalos, there were pine groves sacred to the god Pan, who had loved her as an Oread nymph, never forsook his love, for all that she fled and took this form in her escape to thwart his hanker. It's not the reverence of antiquity, but it does seem... an echo of it, down the ages. Sacred to Dionysus, the Aleppo pine was still an inspiration aeons later, for Paul Cézanne, moved by his garden in Aix-en-Provence, to put brush to canvas and articulate his ardour in *Les*

Grands Arbres. And still, even now, more aeons and a world away, the echoes still resound.

•

WET SAND, MANILA envelope, cappuccino, dry clay, wrapping paper, Nefertiti's foundation—none of these quite match the colour in hue and lustre, a brown paled to buff but pinked as with embarrassment.

It looks nice, says Jaq. It's like... shy sandstone.

The room is echoey empty to his voice, just the painted walls, the polished floor, and four fleshlings all jiggered, quanked by the sore swink and gaumed with paint, two of them fair spattered to clatty, the lovers roped in to sharpen the shift, make themselves useful for a change, having cabbled in play through the work—*Don't just stand there looking glaikit, dunderhead—Says the gormless galoot—Big numpty—Wee nyaff*—and tipped the banter into full-on rammy shenanigans with the spraypacks, until curbed by simultaneous bellows from both Ana and Renart: *Quit it!*

The paint, which it would be an ignorance of haccaeity to call pale brown, is drying to a crust on Jaq's face now, a full face-pack sprayed full brunt, sleeved off to smearage of streaks; and on the wall it is already tacky to the touch; and it is, Ana agrees, a whole lot better, much more her.

Renart brings in now, from the kitchen, the zig-zag chair of Gerrit Rietveld: four square planes of beechwood, dovetail-jointed; back vertical down to z-shape of: seat, diagonal, base: angles crisp as apple crunch. It won't go here, he thinks, but it's ideal for a seat, to study and plan: order, design, composition; tone, form, symmetry; balance: Sondheim chanelling Seurat.

A bedsuite for Ana scientist smoker syrinxist and so on Massinger, who insists that her science is not a reduction of his craft in its abstraction, but an expansion. At the extremes of science we enter poetry, she claims, the purest application of mathematics. Poesis is the suppositional calculus, notated not in symbol but in stance: epistemic; alethic; deontic; boulomaic. And if *she* should be able to see the impossibility of a viable life in a dull grey room, *he* should be able to wrangle a few numbers into sense especially when, look, it's a *glassy* permutation of a Fibonnaci Spiral.

Puk, as Renart is musing, Ana making coffee, and Jaq idling, is weaving this decorative exploit into their gaming of an harpagmos, which required a twofold offering during the course of it—a votive tablet of painted wood, an animal sacrifice—at the sanctuary of Hermes and Aphrodite. The window frame, he has decided, can be their votive tablet turned inside out, object opened to its delineating edges to articulate its reverence with greater import, to make the world itself its prayer.

And there's beef in the chiller, says Jaq. For Ana's chilli. What? It's dead animal.

Which reminds him: Puk needs new togs, Jaq has resolved, and it's his task as erastes to busk his eromenos, bedizen the lad. He starts blethering of Puk comical with trouserlegs rolled up to bare shins, wading in the brook at the bottom of the stead. They could hit the markets if they're surplus now, or if Sifu Renart can savvy the shipshaping of the bedsuite as pronto as Jaq is sure he will.

We need to get you some proper britches, he says.

•

SHE IS THREE in one, Karya, a trinity of sisters, English walnut flanked by hazelnut and sweet chestnut, *Juglans regia* flanked by *Coryllus avellana* and *Castanea vesca*, wearing the same name in all three guises to the Greeks who harvested from all three types of nut tree, this triune aspect an echo perhaps of the two sisters who schemed viciously to thwart a Lakonian maiden's dalliance with Dionysus, and were driven mad for it, fled up the scree slopes of Mount Taygetos where they were turned to stones, while she herself, dying, was changed into a deciduous tree growing twenty-five to thirty-five metres tall, her male flowers drooping catkins which fruit in autumn with green fleshy husks around the edible nut, her summer canopies now lining the Avenue K. Leslie Steiner, shattering the sunlight as Susurrus dances her, to dapple

Jaq and Puk and a gaggle of skimbooted kidsters who zip past them, whooping.

The goddess Artemis told her dad Dion of the unfortunate affair, insisted that he found a sanctuary in honour of Artemis Karyatis. So, at Karyai in Lakonia, in her sacred grove of walnut or hazelnut trees, she had priestesses known as Karyatides, this sisterhood of the nut tree immortalised: in the porch of the Erechthion on the Acropolis in Athens, in stone canephora carrying baskets on their heads full of sacred foods for the goddess's feast, each pillar of individuality carved with its own face, hair, drapery and stance; and in similar stone caryatids down the ages, in Classical Rome, Renaissance Italy, Northern Mannerism.

As if every walnut tree were not a caryatid, and each tree unique, as here, along the whole length and on both sides of the avenue of shops and stalls the lovers stroll, these stately rows of verdant pillarings a ceremonial sorority in procession, leading back the way erastes and eromenos came, to the little dogleg of Stroedeker and the culvert off it, to the townhouse doorstep and a newly dedicated sanctuary more sacred than the grandest temple in its modest unpretension, as a home.

•

I'M NOT REALLY much for cooking, says Ana.

She slices the ends off an onion and peels, brown flakes of dry papery crunkle falling away, retaining curvature on the counter where they're tossed, the smoother layer beneath stripping bit by bit under a thumbnail and scowl, to naked pearl white. She halves the whole now, lays each half flat, and slices, this half first—each knifecut through the pale crump of strata as crisp as the air is, sharp acidic waft watering eyes—then the next. Rough methodical chopping of the fanning slices, and the odd stray chunk firing out tiddlywinks from under blade, serve as a *no comment* on her self-assessment. Satisfied, she grabs a wooden spoon and takes the plateful to the pot, swipes the lot into a sizzle of olive oil, stirs.

Renart, as she stirs up the sizzle to a slowly richening aroma, as the onions shift imperceptibly gradually toward translucence, is still pottering on about his work, lumping gubbins dumped in Puk's room or the hall, sometimes the kitchen, through to the master bedsuite, rapt in his task to a *Scoobedy-doop-doop, bibbedy-bap* absent and elsewhere mode of focus. In his element, it seems.

She dumps the diced steak in, to another sizzle, stirs, stirs and returns to the chopping board.

One sweet red pepper, one orange pepper, both cut vertically from the stem, down and around and back up, to be cracked open and have the seeds stripped and shaken and teased out with a finger. She returns to tumble the browning beef roughly with the spoon, flick a morsel over here or there.

Scoob, scoobedy-doobedy, doo-bow. Smells nice.

Four jalapeños, two green, two red, one of each finely diced, one of each sliced. These she takes to the pot and adds. Another stir, digging under with the spoon to shovel, fold, checking for blood red, turning.

Off in the bedsuite again, Renart folds togs and shelves them, carving some cunning system, no doubt, that will put all to hand, as she dresses of a morn, with the precision of some antique knight's squire sprung to buckle armour; but Susurrus leaves him to it, is more attentive to the cooking, relishing the shift of it in him, the tickle of air currents spiraled from the heat, the tang of oniony steam that seeps him, swirls in him through the kitchen with the open window that invited him inside.

At the cooker, Ana cracks a can of some cheap carbonated drink, full of sugar and spice, pours it gluggling and hissing into the pot—her secret ingredient.

Tum-ti-tum, ti-tum-tum-tum!

Dried chilli flakes sprinkled liberally from a bag. A crush of crimsons and terracottas, seeded with dark and light ochres, it looks like it belongs in the pestle of some ancient artist, to be ground for pigment, mixed with egg yolk and applied to a church wall in tempera fresco, or daubed with a finger on the ceiling of a cave to conjure a bison in silhouette.

The tail of the turkey-cock turns to the sun! Sander of Tempe chanelling Stevens.

A carton of chopped tomatoes. A carton of kidney beans. A stir. A step back, a release of breath, halfway a stance of satisfaction at a dusted job, halfway a momentary daze, as if at a loss as to what to do now, or in suspicion of loose ends left. She looks at Renart, who stands in the kitchen doorway.

Well, she says, it just has to simmer now. Won't be done for a yonk.

•

WHAT DO YOU think? Am I prepped for action?

Jaq in Puk's skivvies, pinging waistband and thumbing thighbands straight, rootling pod to set his bollocks, shift cock to the left. To the right.

I don't know which way I dress, he says. These are yanked.

He settles on upright as fated outcome anyway given stirrings to the novel cling and intimacy of frottage by proxy, or loinspace incursion, or whatever it is that's scrunching ballsack and rousing yen in his pintle. Yen that earns dints of esteem from other browsers in the togstore, an invite from a gazing ageling girl over by the hats, which he dints thanks and apologies to, sorry, he forgot to update his publics with his tweaked kinsey, which she missives a shame, them both being sixers, but sweet that he'd do that for his beau, shift his hanker to fit so snug, and no need to apologise at all. Also: his gambit to unspotlight Puk is *adorable*, if he doesn't mind her saying.

Puk having been blithe to strip in the store, since Erehwynan nonchalance was on display throughout among the browsers—no different to the sauna, really—but unprepped for the sprucer those browsers were politely nudged to cleanse with before trialling summer-sweaty skin in whatnot. Heads turned to his yelp of startle, from the cubicle, at the blasts of high-pressure vapour from all angles, and hot air to dry, and focused particularly on nooks of flesh most like to be ripe. And of course the door opened auto the click it was done, so there Puk stood, mortified by the pricking of his pintle at the sprucer's intimacies. Whereupon Jaq, fingersnap pronto, tossed him the first britches to hand, (navy blue,) nimble as could be, and dropped his own in a grand diversionary show of trialling this quaint custom of underwear, with a quick stride down the aisle a few steps, as if to optimise Puk's view of his twirl, but in fact to set a precise distance whereby they weren't a duo drawing more attention now, but rather a soloist and his singular but backgrounded audience.

Try the paisley, he says, the black on silver. It'll be like a flip of your Geister synthe, a Fourier Harmony.

It's not about transforming Puk to a native, Jaq explains as the Earther slips out of one set of britches and into the other, or painting him as a sham of such, but about finding the permutation of him for this new domain.

How about these ones? says Puk.

The same pattern in crimson and jade.

Even better, says Jaq.

•

HERBACEOUS, RHIZOMATOUS, PERENNIAL, *Mentha spicata* (or *viridis*) sprouts well in most any temperate climate, from her fleshy rhizome spreading wide and down into the soil—unless some spoilsport gardener captures her invasive roots in pots or planters—stretching her variably hairless to hairy stems from thirty centimetres to a metre tall in limber abundance. She does prefer partial shade, she has made it clear to Susurrus, but will thrive in anything from mostly shade to full sun, flourishing soft leaves with serrated margins, five to nine centimetres long, one and a half to three centimetres broad, the oil of spearmint chewed from her tender pale green flesh by Puk now, from a soggy leaf lipped from a straw, rich with the dextro-carvone which imbues her aromatic foliage with that scent so unmistakeably fresh it was only natural to use her on the bodies of the dead, to hold the line valiantly (if vainly) against the stench of rot. Used as a treatment for hirsutism in women too, spearmint produces flowers in slender spikes, each flower pink or white, a slight two and a half to three millimetres long and broad.

She has always been pretty, in sight, scent, taste. The god Hades loved his Minthê for that, and she basked in his affections, blithe until the day she boasted in her pride that she was *so* much better than his queen Persephone, at which the goddess, or her mother Demeter perhaps, transformed the nymph into the mint plant they'd then use to flavour the sacred barley-drink of their Eleusinian Mysteries, as she would one day flavour also, in far western lands of slaves, mint juleps and mojitos, which taste much better here, in a tavern on Boulevard Hovendaal, in the mouths of dark and golden-eyed lovers. Taste best in each other's mouths as they kiss in the recessed booth, Jaq fumbling with the tash on Puk's trews, unbuttoning the ballop, because when the tumblespace cast danced focus from a pairing in the New Davenport outlet to frame the snugged lushes, Puk gave an *oh! oh!* and a grinning handflap, and pounced to mash lips, to whoops and whistles of esteem.

•

DAWNLIGHT THROUGH THE door of the treehouse.

The fuzzled canoodling that inflamed, via gropes and giggles, opposed by half-hearted remonstrations from Jaq that he was far too soused, advanced, by resolute demonstrations from Puk that Jaq's tadger was not, through frolic to hard fuckery is now reprised as mawmsey croodling, the two well-fucked and well-fadged in the after, snuggling still socketed. Warm breath on the back of his neck, canty in Jaq's couthy embrace, Puk yawns as he drumbles how their socketing feels designed.

Getting back is a blur: a stumbling carouse along Steiner to cadge a hitch, Jaq's brainpop scheme, from one of the nightcarters offloaded now at Bradshaw Market, headed back out through the subrurals, and ever resolute to grant passage on request, ever a seat kept free in their skimcart, in memory of the flight from Phobos's shattering, a custom deep as oath: never again to have no room for one asking transport; Puk on Jaq's lap squirming drunk and hyper to grope and clumse Jaq's doublet free from a ferntickled shoulder, to show it—see?—his Phobian ancestry; midway in the weavy stagger after being dropped, along the long empty winds through forestry pitch black either side, paths carved in the gleam of asphalt below, the star-strewn and fob-scythed vault above, stumbling and tumbling in a crash into thick burdock, lying on his back, looking up at the vastation of that abyss, atramentine and asparkle; puking at the side of the road; being *Nearly there, nearly there;* taking a slug of rum from a flask magicked by Jaq from who knows where; being recovered and rannigant again enough, when at last they made it to the stead, that he flailed free of sensible steerage toward Jaq's room, and went crash splashing prancing off in a run through undergrowth like a kidster in surf, to their oak and elm, calling Jaq to him like a mutt, cracking up at it; and the two clambered up into the treehouse to flop in a tangle, frisky Puk wrappling Jaq back out of laze and into lusty yen.

So they fucked wild, Puk astride at first, then turned, to his hands and knees, to be tupped under Jaq's hunching thrusts, hips and shoulder and fists of hair yanked back, for the prick to ram jam bam and cram him, till he felt it fill him, and he'd swear to cock, the jism spouted into and through him and out his own spurting prick.

And now, here they lie on their sides, snuggling still socketed, Puk blissed to feel Jaq inside and around him as he gazes out at dawnlight through the door of the treehouse.

VI

•

Academic of theosophical Sufi, in his essay, "Mundus Imaginalis, or The Imaginary and the Imaginal," Henry Corbin paints the landscape of an alterior realm of subtle bodies, an altjeringa of archetypes, Islamic, Jungian, Platonic. Stancing the *imaginal,* as he calls it, *independent of any substratum in which it would be immanent in the manner of an accident,* he comes so so close to unmasking the projectivity that guises as eternity, but ultimately surrenders to the mystical, the metaphysical. What he needs is Jarry's science, *extending as far beyond metaphysics as the latter extends beyond physics,* the science of imaginary solutions, attributing the traits of objects to their lineaments.

Yeats's Byzantium, Joyce's Dublin, Lorca's Andalucia: a moorish wall, a wall, any wall. In sailing *from* the Byzantium of metaphysics, pataphysics returns us to the material, the moment; it simply approaches from a new direction, scrutinising the real in terms of the shift and span of time rather than its stint. Transpositions to analogue alterities of space and stint may be (must be?) conjured by the pataphysicist, as physicists conjure flavour and colour in a quark, but if we are not talking of the shift and span of the substance of *this* realm, the existential, then our pataphysics has crumbled back to the false infinities and infinitesimals of spiritualism and semiotics, the superstitions of soul and sign.

So, Corbin crumbles back to the Cartesian homunculi of

metaphysical soul or intellect, equivalent nonsenses of nous as puppeteer, when he stances imagination the interface to this realm, a third capacity between *sense* and *intelligence,* as if there was a difference. Intelligence is sense; ideas have their taproots in impressions, as Hume traced. Meanwhile, sense is intelligence; the visual import of blue as gleaned from any flower—Hyacinth's actual bloom, Novalis's romantic emblem, Hume's putative unseen—is not an inherent quality of light but rather a stance in the blue-yellow opponent process, the percept always already a concept, a note as arbitrary in its relation to the real as the scents of hyacinth to benzyl acetate, indole and phenylacetaldehyde.

There is no utopia for subtle bodies, no *out of nature*: the pataphysique is animal flesh; the pataphysical realm is blood-stained soil, a field of poppies; both are matter being seen from another temporal angle.

This is what Ana is trying to explain to Renart, who of all people should savvy, his very craft the hammering of bodily form, the work of Yeats's goldsmith sailed back from Byzantium to the real, the downright *psychophysiological.* How can the artisan, finally returned from aeons in fantasia, his sleeves rolled up, ready to fashion us the bold and beautiful pataphysiques we've all along been yearning for, not wrapple the notion of agencies emergent in the pataphysical reticulum *without* collapsing it to *animist mumbo jumbo?*

Renart can only shrug surrender, hands empty of explanation. He works at the human level, engineer of affect, fouterer with the gubbins of sensation. He can only savvy her work in metaphors, as an anthropology of dryads living in the trees. Computational analyses of synchronicitous patterning in physical super-systems... to him that just means number-crunching chaos till you find what you're looking for, footsteps of gods that don't exist.

They *don't* exist, says Ana. She's talking about echoes in shift, shadows in span, things that only translate, mathematically translate, into stories. He doesn't understand.

Breezing across the surface of the world outside, the godling of the Martian winds, son of Zephyrus and terraformed Ares, Susurrus understands.

•

Swipper and whippety, Jaq dreeps down from a branch of Baucis, loosing with a swing to land smackdab on the basalt fo'c'sle in a superhero crouch steadied with one fist, barely a slap on the rock underfoot but with a stramash of ramage springing back above that sets the white flash of a rabbit's scut bouncing off into the grass of his sward. Nekkid but for Puk's Geister jerkin, and all the more nekkid for it, he's followed sharpish by Puk in britches of paisley, crimson and jade, more daredevil than Jaq's monkeyboy poise: a running jump, whooping, from the treehouse itself, arms windmilling in air, bold in his Earther frame and scorn of Martian gravity, landing with a crump into a roll in the grass beyond the rock—more a spill than roll, really, which ends with him on his back, but still, a sound trumping by courage, if not poise, and rivalling in gusto, setting them equal over all, in Shim's reckoning, which both with magnanimity dispute, good heathens that they are, each declaring the other victor, not from self-abasement but from mutual esteem and, in no small part, ardour.

Jaq, sauntered from the rock to offer a hand, insists. Puk, latching grasp and hauling himself up to his feet, contends.

It is precisely many weeks, days and hours into the harpagmos—*many* being the most accurate measure for time fluttered by in stints made immeasurable in the warp of shift and span, days of fuckery passing in a tick, idle hours lazed in the grass, playing Fourier Harmonies, stretching wide as a starscape. A wheen weeks and a pochle of days now for the two whiffets maybe, but who's to say? Without a stick to cut a chack in for every moment of weight worth tally, a mere clockware call for stint would be inaccurate.

Arbiter of the exploit, Shim leans sideways on the trunk of Philemon, Don behind with an arm crooked round her waist, chin on her shoulder; Joi lounges with arms folded, back to Baucis: Jaq's cohort popped by on an excursion from Erehwyna to see how the cretins are getting on, haven't seen them for yonks, do they want to come snoop the old mines in Euripus Mons? They wander out from under the shade, to a new disposition on the rock: Don hopped atop it, thumbs tucked in his britches; Shim seated slantways with an arm as prop; Joi with one leg up, leaning forearm on thigh. The cretins don't *have* to come, if they're busy being cretins, but it'll be peachy, spooky in the depths, and there's the paintings left during the Interregnum.

Glances between Puk and Jaq, one antsy and awkward, one curious and double-taking to scry, then Jaq blinks and hedges that they *did* have plans which they could drop but... He almost dints Joi private that some snag in the scheme's a panicky no-no for his matelot, ixnay, but Joi twigs it anyway, or savvies the tact here at least, and smoothly brushes it no bother, just a whim while passing. So instead they crack some beers from the treehouse stash—because *hospitality*—savour a few ticks of catching up, then Jaq's cohort scoot, leaving the cretins to their fun.

Cretans, says Jaq.

Don grins, tips a wink and a wave, and they're off.

And after, the gusto of cameraderie is such that the moment of fret seems history to Puk, scrambling up the rope ladder for another beer, and Jaq's tenty to broach it. A phobia? They're both unlocked to each other's privates, quirks declared as kinsey and hanker. Ah well. He notes to keep edgy for hints, and when Puk's eased he'll savvy Jaq, he's sure, in time. Whatever it is.

Susurrus knows, felt it in the prickle of hair on the back of Puk's neck, how their Greek idyll clicked with mineshaft depths, and snicked three striplings round a rock to an image out of Poussin, a whiplash thought of tombs, and of stone collapsing, crushing, killing: et in arcadia ego. And it wasn't a fear for himself. That would've been fine.

Catch! cries Puk from the crow's nest treehouse, and Jaq catches the beer one-handed.

•

THE BLACK POPLAR, Dryope, *Populus nigra,* is a middling-large deciduous tree, reaching thirty metres tall, with a bole diameter of one and a half metres, her bark the grey-brown of a dusty elephant's hide, thick furrowed, heavy burred, trunk sloping as if to reach, not *up* to the gods, the sun or sky, no, not fastigiate as elsewhere, but reaching *over* as to some other on the ground. Perhaps to the two fleshlings lazing in the ryegrass.

In Poland, her shoots and leaves, rhomboid to cuneate, five to eight centimetres long, six to eight centimetres broad, were glabrous. Here, subspecies betulifola of Western Europe, they carry a fine down. Dioecious, she flowers in catkins, is pollinated by the wind, by Susurrus, who snakes round her even now as Apollo did, once or twice, far ago, shape-shifting from the tortoise she was charmed by, that she laid on her lap as she fell asleep, only to awake in the windings of that serpent, yes, Apollo, sire of her son, Amphissus, who she was suckling some nine months and a little later as she wandered by a lake one day and came upon a lotus tree.

She picked a bloom for her son to play with. The tree trembled, bled an ichor that rooted her to the spot the moment it touched her skin, transforming her from the feet up. Her husband sprinted to her frantic cries, arrived in the nick of time to snatch Amphissus from her arms, mark her plea to raise him never, never, never to pick flowers.

She may still be reaching for him, still pleading. She may be reaching out to the fleshlings.

•

JAQ PUFFS, SCATTERING to Susurrus the umbel of a dandelion, lying on his back, watching parachutes of seed and pappus drift away into the blue.

If you touch the juice seeping from the stem of a plucked dandelion, says Puk beside him, it means you'll pee the bed. In French, dandelions were known as *pissenlit*, in English *pissabeds*. Dandelion is derived from *dent-de-lion,* teeth of the lion. *Taraxacum oficinale*. It is actually a diuretic.

A few bracts picked, Jaq flicks the stalk away, rolls away to pluck another flower, then heaves up to straddle him, tap him on the nose with this other bloom and trail it down over lips, under chin.

If you hold a buttercup, he says, *Ranunculus repens*, under the anterior belly of someone's digastric muscle, like this, and the sunlight reflected just so bathes the jut of jaw with a golden glow... it means they like butter.

Coyote's makeshift eyes, says Puk. One day he was throwing them up in the air and catching them, showing off, and Eagle came down and snatched them. So he had to improvise, grab the first thing that came to hand.

Facts or fictions, neither is telling the other anything they need to hear, not in the words.

When all knowledge is not just at your fingertips but in them, in a hangnail or a nip of keratin eponchyium, little claw snag gnawed in nerves or idling, sliver pricking lip or tongue for a second then spit *ptooey* to riverside sedge, rushes underfoot, before you grab rough hemp, kick back and swing out on the knot-end of a rope to whooping whirl of limbs and cannonball *sploosh*, not caring that you can't skinnydip in the same river twice says Herakleitos; when you only have to need a fact for the PAN in your frown of brow to pinch it for you from the hylenet, slip it into your nous, then:

All schooling is a matter of stance.

•

White poplar, *Populus alba,* she was named Leukippe as a girl, Leuke for short, most beautiful of all Oceanid nymphs, mirror of Persephone, carried off by Hades to live out her natural in his domain. Hell holds no fear for her then, not now, not here. How to face the fleeting of life is as clear as the shouts of boys she hears riding Susurrus far ahead of nekkid flesh, the holler of wheeling wildlimbs careening down slope of sward, race braked only at the crash through copse so they can chimpwalk across the log of an elder her now fallen, bridging the burn to the other bank, the water-meadow that is one edge of their summer's domain, at which she waits.

She is dioecious, rust red stamens on male catkins on another tree, grey-green of female catkins on this, produced months back in early spring. Pollinated now, maturing with the turn of late spring to early summer, already lengthening to nigh on ten centimetres, forming the green seed capsules. Sneakily, she is also trying to propagate herself with root suckers sprouting from her lateral roots, dreaming of the clonal colony she may form, binding the sandy soil of the burn's bank as she does so. She might make the whole slim river an avenue all the way to where it joins the Rio Erehwyreve. She delights, as noted by Horace, to grow by the riverbank. Why? It was by the Acheron in the Elysium Fields that Hades transformed her upon death. It was by the Acheron in Thespratia where a Herakles fresh from that same underworld found her foresting the Aventine Hill on his way to slay fire-breathing cannibal giant Cacus, lurking like Australopithicus in a cave lined with skulls of his victims. Great Herakles squeezed the very blood from the ogre's throat, popped his eyes from their sockets with his grip, the sort of feat admired by boys such as these now sprinting for the finish line of her trunk

She is a middling-sized deciduous tree, her trunk up to a metre in diameter, crown broad and rounded, seldom higher than sixteen to twenty seven metres. Young shoots and infant buds are downed with white-grey, just as the five-lobed leaves of four to fifteen centimetres in length sport a thick white scurfy down, which wears off the upper but not the underside, where it is thicker, staying white until the leaves fall in the autumn. It was from these leaves double-sided green and white as life and death that Herakles wove a crown for himself to celebrate his deed. All athletes after, in games sacred to Herakles or in funeral games—because all funerals should have games joyful as the Olympics at Elis where she was the only wood used in sacrifices to Zeus—all athletes in such games wore wreaths not of laurel but of her, in victory.

The stripling-limbed victor of these two, now slapping a hand on her trunk and crowing, he should have his eromenos weave such a crown. It would look magnificent on hair as leonine as Herakles's Nemean togs, over a face carnelian as the blood of Cacus's defeat.

His hand, as he steps back, brushes down over dark diamond-shaped marks on her smooth pale, grey-green bark, inverse of scales, so neat they seem diagonal tiles cut out by some wayward scrapbooker with a scalpel. They are just her though, wholly natural. All that is not her is the hemp rope that the fleshling grabs now, scuffling, slipping, springing, with a backkick off the balls of his feet, off toes almost, to swing out, whooping. And even that she is not sure of. Even that feels a part of who she is.

•

THE PHANTOMS ARE not AIs, Ana explains, neither *artifice* nor *intelligence* being adequate notions for the quirks of corrade and collage she's studying, these emergent sentiences wrought in slow accretions of shift, mycelial plethora of span.

You frame phantoms as genuine agents, says Renart, but geists...

The corpse rotting in its grave shifts more than the geist, she says, and the geist has no span, nada. Too much like us and not enough.

Her stance brooks no quibbling. Such a black and white view Renart might tend to counter—a brockit view is a broken one, he's like to say—but he's no hanker to tempt her fire. In the Massinger homestead, now hued and honed to her throughout, seated on the Rietveld chairs at the kitchen table under the window, bustle of outside wafting in on Susurrus, picking at pomegranate seeds she wouldn't hear of him declining, she clicks as Erehwynan as any, but it's clear she inherits her father's thrawn resolve, which he, by all accounts, inherited from his own, only with a flip out of zealot and into rebel.

It's the new mirror test, far as I'm concerned, she says. Anyone who can't see the scission between self and geist? Isn't a self.

Harsh stance, says Renart. Surely if it plays like a self, you're as well to stance it back as one.

He doesn't say, but he lost a sister as a kidster, long ago now, can see the solace in a geist, not in the fancy of eternity, but as a remembrance, to visit and chat with years on, after the fading of grief.

See? That's why I'm a pataphysicist and you're a pataphysician. Creatives, she shakes her head.

•

Cultivated in archaic orchards with the apple and the pear, the fig and olive, *Punica granatum*, pomegranate, is a small deciduous tree or shrub which grows to a height of five to eight metres, bearing a fruit around the size of an orange, red with a juicy red pulp, rich in blood red seeds that once, as signifiers of female fertility, made it an attribute of Hera, goddess of marriage, fruit of Aphrodite too, but prohibited as food for initiates in the mysteries of Demeter and Persephone, the latter of whom had stubbornly refused to eat at all while hostage and unwilling fiancé of the underworld king, until sly Hades tempted her with pomegranate seeds and, finally relenting while he'd wandered off or looked away, Persephone took the bait and sprung the trap upon herself, Askalaphos, keeper of the pomegranate orchards of the netherworld, reporting to his master that she'd tasted of the seed, the poor girl then condemned to spend a part of every year in this dismal domain, albeit Askalaphos reaped his own unsweet reward at the hands of Demeter, who turned him to a screech owl perching on the branches of the first fruit tree of his own orchard, the very pomegranate sent to Hades from the goddess Hera, in metamorphic punishment for having boasted herself more beautiful than the very bride of Zeus, one day, back when she wore her own flesh, as she lay abed with her great hunter husband, giant Orion and, snuggling into her, he whispered her name: Sidê.

•

I'm sorry, says Jaq. I'm really... I didn't mean it.

Puk tromps ahead through pinnate fronds, feet thrashing furious.

I'm sure it's not him, says Jaq helplessly. I didn't think.

On a tree stump, twigs sprouting round the wirrocks in what trunk rose stunty out of thick roots, Jaq spotted the grey-brown ball of an owl pellet, bone and fur, poked it with the twig he'd been chewing and joshed he could glean, in the ruin of it, music, poetry, philosophy, astronomy, mathematics, and science—Apollo Sminthius, you see, mouse god on Tenedos.

Where are you going? Please, I'm sorry.

As fust or oose on a rotting fruit in a still life, it seemed only a natural shading of this vital summer they've been living, part of the game of Greek idyll—elegy an inherent aspect; but he savvied even before done blurting that he'd dropped into a ravine, all but dangling a dead mouse in Puk's face and dubbing it Apple. Idiot. And before he'd even yanked himself from the wreckage of realisation and all the potential pointless fumbles to explain that sprang instant to his nous, to just pour out abject horror at being a graceless witless boor, Puk was already through aghast and hurt and enraged, and simply away.

Jaq hurries after him, still pleading at first, quieting as Puk crashes on through the ferns, his back a wall of cold wrath, set to it speaking of something beyond placations, something placations will only further incense. When the stint of this stretches beyond mere huff, Jaq twigs that *something* deeper than he savvies, twigs that he needs to just give space to whatever it is, so he lets himself drift behind. Stops when Puk does, at the river's edge. Waits. Eventually, that something eases its ineffable complexity to simple anger, and a while after that Puk turns, comes stalking up to him.

Why would you even say that?

Jaq, currently two to four centimetres small, point five centimetres slight or less, bearing on his glabrous, downcast face a heavy inflorescence of shame, carrying some dozen seeds of self-rebuke, and when crushed, as now, exuding a distinct aroma of regret, doesn't know.

Why? Why would you even say that?

He didn't think.

It's enough to win an amnesty of sorts: a punch in the arm and a silent return, Jaq in tow, to the treehouse; a few hours of brooding on one side and reserve on the other; a tense foray into the stead for grub with Renart tactfully ignoring the atmosphere; then eventually, later, a long conversation that clears the air with explanations, apologies, forgiveness and not a word from either of the two on the actual raw wound Jaq accidentally reopened.

•

He was a titan once, Sykeus, *Ficus carica,* the edible fig, one of that ancient race who ruled before the gods, rammied with them in the first great war. When it smacked him in the face he was on the losing side, he fled from Zeus through time itself, finding refuge from the king god's lightning wrath in transformation at the hands of Gaia in one aeon, Demeter in another. The goddess of the earth was resting from her weary search for Persephone, you see, having been offered shelter by a kindly Phytalos, when Sykeus leapt out of the war and into sight, as luck would have it, just as she was casting round for some way to reward her host.

So, she snatched Sykeus from the aether and transformed him to a fig tree, planted him there for Phytalos in the early Neolithic village of Gilgal I, in the Jordan Valley, thirteen kilometres north of Jericho, where nine subfossil figs of a parthenocarpic type would eventually be found and dated to around 9400–9200 BCE. That one who was once a Titan should retain such deep antiquity seems fit, Susurrus reckons. Predating the domestication of barley and legumes, one thousand years before humanity tamed wheat and rye, that find of Sykeus's intentional planting and cultivation back on Earth, back before Susurrus was even sprung, stanced itself to be the first known instance of agriculture, and given the scouring and rebuilding of the old world in the aeons since, that find seems now unlikely to be easily usurped. If there are older tamings undiscovered, only gods and titans know.

He may not be a titan now, but Sykeus still has fair stature against the fleshlings, growing to a height of twenty-three to thirty-three feet tall, with smooth grey bark beneath which, in the green parts, lies a sap that acts as irritant to human skin. His leaves are twelve to twenty-five centimetres long and ten to eighteen centimetres wide, and deeply lobed with three or five lobes. Three to five centimetres long, the fruit has a green skin which sometimes ripens towards purple or brown, as if to hint at the imperial might of gods or the chthonic brawn of titans, at king's robes and warlord's leathers.

•

A GEIST IS just, as far as Ana is concerned, the clay-fleshed skull of an ancestor shelved in some home shrine of Çatal Huyuk, a clockwork calliope built into the wall behind, a library of stances coded in pianola rolls that are switched by the keys we press, so steam whistling through the lips seems to voice the persona of the dead.

She pauses for breath as she sets the bowl of figs down on the table.

You never bought it? says Renart.

Raised outside the faith, she says. But that doesn't mean outside the law.

Her parents didn't want to be geisted at all, but estrangement from the Geister fellowship meant nada to a federal law favouring the doctors' oath over the most ardent layman's testament. So, after the accident, the gleaning and upload went ahead, with Ana protesting all the way to New Jerusalem, and there they were in the Ancestry, the geists of Fellows Mona and Hari Massinger.

It's not us, was the first thing they said.

Your mother's geist isn't going to lie to you, is it? Not if she wasn't lying to herself in life.

That's what the other geists are doing, she says, stancing delusions copied into them, going through the motions of belief. It sickens her, generations of cowards taking echoes of their forebears' fears as proof. Everything is ephemeral, every *some*thing anyways. Only anything persists.

•

MINGLING JASMINE AND hyacinth, the scent of Narkissos, *Narcissus poeticus*, or Poet's Daffodil, is heady enough to cause headaches and nausea, even vomiting in over-abundance. Still, the essential oil has its use in perfumes and, *being laid on with Loliacean meal and honey*, Dioscorudes claimed, in his Materia Medica, *it draws out splinter*s.

Not just a pretty face then, Narkissos. Though he does have a pretty face, even now, from a stem twenty to forty centimetres high, blooming a single flower, with a short corona in light yellow edged with red, his perianth having three white sepals to the calyx, three white petals to the corolla.

Of all the flowers and shrubs and trees who were once human, Narkissos reckons himself the most familiar in all likelihood, a whole pathology of egoism named for his cautionary tale of a lad who wasted away sat on a riverbank, mooning over the unattainable beauty of his own reflection, or leaning over to kiss his image, falling in and drowning. It is a beautiful poetic tale, he likes to think, painted through the ages less in caution than in melancholy, all those artists understanding the acute yen for a union with the imago of self, seeing in him not the folly of shallow vanity, but rather the projection out into the world of this ephebic symbol of the soul, a recognition of the way the world returns to us, if we gaze upon it as a mirror, the beauty of our humanity, and oh, what it is to look upon, to see the soul in a river looking back at you, to see the potential of perfection; is there any way to not yearn for a fusion with the ideal?

That's where the true tragedy is, he says, that I was right to love and want this image of the perfect self, that it is exquisitely to be wished for; but even as we surrender to the rapture of our grace, we are bound in flesh, so ephemeral, so delicate, creatures who waste or drown, ever starving and ever gasping, unless and until translated to some eternal form as, say, a flower with a white trinity of petals.

Sure, says Susurrus. If you say so.

Truth be told, he thinks the Poet's Daffodil has a worse case of self-love than any narcissist was ever diagnosed with, might have found his ideal more attainable if it *included* eating... and looked a little wider or a little deeper than the face upon the surface of the water; but the precious blossom is unconscionably pretty, so Susurrus tholes the whole hand-nailed-to-forehead fantasy to flirt, to brush by with a saucy stroke that makes Narkissos shiver. Still, after only a few minutes tickle and twirl, such wishful double-thinking always makes his head hurt and his stomach churn, as it's doing now, so he gives a last curl of a kiss and slips away, leaving the flower where he grows, down by the river's edge, where Puk stood earlier that day, (or maybe yesterday? or last week?) fuming in an inarticulable stance, racked from raw bone-and-flesh experience of the ephemeral, that Narkissos has no sense or savvy of, and no salve for. Too big a splinter, thinks Susurrus.

He was strewn on graves, Narkissos, back on Earth, back in antiquity, because Persephone was gathering a posey of his blossoms on the day that Hades took her. Pretty flowers for a grave, thinks Susurrus, but... as if the stench of the rotting dead needs made more vomitous. And he has to wonder if perhaps the god of the dead was drawn out by that smell.

VII

•

The second of three set scenes in vase paintings of the erastes-eromenos relationship, as classed by Beazley, is the presentation of a small gift, often hares or roosters, sometimes deer or cats. None of these being wholly practical for Jaq to filch or Puk to tend—except cats, on which subject Jaq agrees with his Diogenes: they're just plain *wrong*—Puk hadn't, he admits, really expected more than the symbolic here. Sat on the basalt rock with Jaq at his back, he chomps a bite of soft pear, talks through the noms: really he'd been prepped for a sim like the cup, or a wordplay on cock most like. *That*, he says, was neat.

That morn, Puk woke to a prod in his shoulder socket, prod, prod, and a hand over his mouth stifling mumbley yawn, blinking bleary to focus on Jaq's face afore him, finger to lips. Slowly drawn away and, with slightest move, crooked to point down the valley between them, toward the treehouse door. Where, just inside, a mouse nosed the floorboards, frecking a scamper and twitch around, this way and that, in murine questing, bold as a brat till Puk shuffled in perk and sparked a dash, a scurrying straight for escape and gone.

Apple, said Puk, sitting up. Well... maybe.

Had to wake you, said Jaq. I was fretted your snores would scare him off.

Jaq's impression, half pig snort, half donkey bray, won a slap.

Then thanks, Puk gazing after the scarpered rodent, asmile at the small gift of a glimpse, Apple or otherwise. Frau Apple, Apple Junior, First Apple Twice Removed, it's enough that *this* little bundle of bone and fur is still quick.

So now, Puk wipes the pear juice from his lips—a Starkrimson, bud mutation of Clapp's Favourite, its creamy flesh sweet and aromatic, its skin thick and smooth and red, deeper red than Jaq, same sard as Puk himself almost. Or it was, nom nom. He hops himself down from the rock, winds back as a catchball pitcher at the serve, and whiplashes, hurling the core out over the sward, high and far. Wipes hands on britches.

Show off, says Jaq.

Puk ganders Jaq on the rock, propped on his arms, lounged back with one leg up, one out, naked today rather than nekkid; he flicks a nod of sorts, a sideways back *c'mere;* and Jaq does the puzzled mutt head-cock thing that Puk hunches he understudied Diogenes on, deliberately. (Jaq's thesis, blithely resolute: Paleolithic domestication by dogs rather than of them; anthropomorphism is really caninomorphism, see, bald apes having learned to project upon themselves such doggy traits as loyalty, exuberance. You don't really believe that, do you? Absolutely!)

What? says Jaq.

Third scene, says Puk.

And Jaq, with a grin, clambers forward, hops down as Puk unlashes his britches, slides them off his hips. The third of three set scenes in vase paintings of the erastes-eromenos relationship, as classed by Beazley, is the consummation.

Standing? says Jak.

Ouais, standing, intercrural, AKA the *sumata* of the Samurai, the *Oxford Style*, the *Princeton First-Year*, the *Ivy League Rub*. Good enough for ensigns of industry, Shaka Zulu, Alexander the Great. The *Altercatio Ganymedis et Helene* has Zeus extoll the slippery thighs of a boy, as Billy Greene swooned over Lincoln's, as perfect as a human being could be, he said.

Streaks of lavender, says Jaq, spots soft as May violets. Ouias.

•

True Myrtle, *Myrtus communis*, Myrsine to her friends, she is a tender evergreen shrub or small tree, reaching up to five metres tall, as Aphrodite found most useful when, one day, she was caught naked on the Isle of Cytheraea, casting round in shame for any sort of hiding place. Myrsine stepped up to the mark, blithe to oblige the goddess, who was often seen from that day on with myrtle leaves around her, each leaf entire, a dense dark green, three to five centimetres long and lanceolate or elliptical, with a fragrant essential oil, a sweet and spicy aroma when bruised or crushed—a reward from Aphrodite, who held her as a favourite for that kind deed, decreed that Myrsine should be evergreen and ever so aromatic, that worshippers should plant her round their temples. Some gossipy sorts spread rumours that she was a priestess of the love goddess, but angered her with a desire to marry a young man she loved, a breach of vows. Nonsense. When she rose from the ocean, Aphrodite wore a wreath of myrtle. Nuff said, really.

The scent and symbol of Eden, in late spring and summer, she is cloaked in wonderfully scented star-shaped flowers, each with five creamy white petals and sepals, and myriad stamens giving her an exotic appearance. These flowers pollinated by insects, the fruit that follows is a round blue-black or purplish berry containing several seeds to be dispersed by birds that eat them and flit away, as far and wide and swift as Myrsine and Athena racing. That's how it really happened: Athena being a sore loser, slaying her in petty spite—and instantly regretting it, turning her body to a myrtle tree in grief and guilt, loving her everafter.

In the islands of Sardinia and Corsica—and so widely known in the former as to be deemed a typical drink—they made an aromatic liqueur by macerating her in alcohol, two varieties, no less: Mirto Rosso from her berries; Mirto Bianco from the leaves. Others were less appreciative of her taste; in Jewish lore the pairing of her pleasant fragrance with unpleasant flavour made her a symbol of those with good deeds to their credit despite a dismal ignorance of the Torah.

Still, that's not so bad, she thinks, and she could hardly be insulted when the pilgrims in Jersualem held three branches of her—three! and only one palm leaf, one citron, even willow rating only two!—as they walked round the Temple, in the ceremonies of Sukkot, the Feast of Tabernacles. To Jewish mystics, meanwhile, she was held a symbol of a phallic force at work throughout the cosmos, virile masculine vitality embodied in a sacred plant; and so her branches would be given to the bridegroom sometimes, at the wedding's end, upon his entry to the nuptial bedsuite.

In England too they saw her flowering as auspicious, augury of wedding in the air. She brings good luck in general, so they said, a healthy myrtle tree or two upon one's land a sign of peace and comfort for one's family, a happy home. She's long been linked with lovers, thought to link them, to inspire love and to make it linger.

She was, if Aristophanes is right, the garland of Iacchus, riotous dancer of the meadows, juggling torches at Eleusis, bringing starlight to the darkness of the rites.

He was right, she says to Susurrus. I remember him. I always liked Iacchus.

And you're sure it's him?

Not literally, of course, but pataphysically? Trust me.

Fingers stretched to brush Myrsine as he passes, tickling her near as flirty as Susurrus, Iacchus Jaq weaves through the brush and shrub, trailblazer to himself if not to Puk, who follows less as an explorer with a native guide, more as a drifter on the raft of Jaq, not at all fussed where they're going or why, simply riding the shiftstream of grass and undergrowth parted as in the wake of a ship.

It is noon. Month, week and day do not matter. It is noon.

•

No, it is five. They have been gathering morels. Where? Under the leaf-laced sky, in the subrural forests far beyond the ambit of Renart's stead, through the cheep of birds, the bummling of bees around a byke nooked in the oxter of a branch, skirting burr thistles, skulking into neighbour's acres to graze fresh-fruited cherries and apricocks, raspberries and strawberries. Whether Puk's sweet tooth or Jaq's colt's tooth was impetus is uncertain, but certainty is overrated anyway.

I'll be your huckleberry, Jaq said, chewing on a fiddlehead of bracken, brushing through a spiderweb while Puk was rubbing a dock leaf on a louping nettle sting.

Now, exploring the carse of the Erehwyreve, around where the bickering burn spreads and slows and flows into the river, Puk is busied in a flail at midges jiggeting the damp brush, air hoaching with them. Now, he misses the dip underfoot and treads shin-deep in a brackish pool slimed with frogspawn. Ick!

Foot splurged deep down into sucking mud, stumbled forward to splash and sink the other foot, he squeals the squeeze of sludge between his toes, the slime gooping legs as he struggles at his bogging, near toppled in imbalance and each foot only sinking more, the more the other rises. Throughout this, Jaq is of course, hooting with laughter, for which Puk, when finally a hand's offered and he's hauled from the muck, gives a mock-sullen *thank you* and then a sudden shove, sending the mocker to poetic justice on his arse.

A handful of spawn scooped and flung, ducked. Puk shrieking as Jaq scrambles out with more, coming for him. The chase is brief and ends with Jaq crowing triumph over a sliming of hair, Puk squeezing out the slick to flick at him, pointing out that Jaq still has the worst of it.

Five, says Puk as they walk on after.

Five what? says Jaq.

An average three thousand eggs laid by a female, and after predation of the tadpoles by goldfish, newts, dragonflies, water beetles and nymphs, and after predation of the frogs by foxes, hedgehogs, rats and who knows what else, maybe five will make it through of the whole brattling of tiddlers.

Five.

•

DAPHNE, *LAURUS NOBILIS,* the laurel, bay tree, sweet bay or bay laurel, grows in a great variety of sizes and heights, sometimes as high as ten to eighteen metres tall, in other places often clipped to a low hedge or, being widely cultivated as an ornamental plant in warmer climates, used in topiary, a single erect stem created with a twisted, spherical or cubic crown. Here on the edge of the stead that Jaq and Puk are skirting, she was once the latter, pruned to a crisp geometry by the novice gardener who, next thing she knew, was famous for his renovation of the Jardins Rochester. Grown wild now for a good while, on the far edge of a stead in ruin, few would twig her as his handiwork these days, but Daphne's fine with that. As crowns go, she's much happier adorning heads of heroes, wishes Puk the best of luck in his browfurrowed trial to weave a wreath for Jaq.

She is evergreen, bearing leaves of six to twelve centimetres long and two to four centimetres broad, with a distinctive margin, wrinkled and finely-serrated. She is dioecious, with male flowers on this plant, female flowers on that, each flower pale yellow-green, around one centimetre in diameter, blooming with a partner beside a glossy green leaf. A glossy sharp green leaf. She really didn't mean to cut his finger; it's just how she is. Well, if he manages to achieve it, even with the glassy how-to gleaned from hylenet scrying, it'll be a victory wreath in every sense.

Her small shiny fruit, a black berry around one centimetre long, one seed within, may be used as a robust spice when dried, as can her pressed leaf oil, while a strong smoke flavoring can be achieved with her burnt wood. A poultice steeped in Daphne's boiled leaves is said to relieve rashes caused by nettles, poison ivy or poison oak; aqueous extracts may be used to salve open wounds or as astringents; while her aromas will alleviate arthritis and rheumatism, hypertension and earaches. Allegedly. As far as Daphne is concerned, she's far more useful as cuisine ingredient—though even cooked her leaves remain so cutting they're best plucked before the dish is served, or ground for use in soups or stocks or Bloody Marys.

Bloody is the word, Susurrus snickers. Bloody fingered. Bloody minded. Bloody—

Shusht, she snips, due credit for the effort, and I'd like to see *you* try, blowhard.

She'll have no mockery of anyone who plays the game. She can't abide gauche winners or spectators jeering clumsy cock-ups. That's her story, after all: Apollo being an insufferable boor, deriding Eros as a rubbish archer, getting shot for it, and suddenly all over her; she ran and fought, and fought and ran, but in the end the only way out was her father Ladon, river god, transforming her to this. Since then... she's never liked smart arses making fun of others. Banter's banter, sport in its own right, but at the Pythian games in Delphi, held in honour of Apollo, where the victor's wreath was made from her, from branches gathered in the Vale of Tempe, Daphne didn't sit upon those winner's heads so they could sneer. That Aristotle fellow had a word for it, you know. He called it—

Magnanimity, Susurrus says. I know.

•

A SMIRR OF rain, sky murkening to iron, charged. The shift of the oncoming summer storm's so palpable, Jaq wonders how the ancients couldn't have the notion—shift, he means. How could they fancy time a one dee stream when they could *see* the gradient in the clouds? Puk dints an image gleaned sharp as a word sprung to the nous from pre-lingistic call: the welter of a van Gogh sky over a wheatfield thick with crows.

Maybe they did, he says. That looks like shift to me.

Ouias, but they tagged *him* mad, says Jaq.

They've strayed far from the stead, delved into wildwoods tracing a tributary of the Erehwyreve that flows down from Euripus. Fir trees edge a gully of sides steep enough they fancy a pre-Interregnum road perhaps cut through, a pathway to the mountain mines. Below, the base is nigh level: rubble of boulders at the base of the rock bank, pebbly, but then mudflats mostly, filmed with water, but the river such that it is mostly just a shallow weave through the centre, higher in winter likely but hardly a torrent to carve a gorge. Up here and on the far bank, all is forest—maybe not so peachy for a storm, says Puk.

Maybe not, says Jaq.

A rimbombo of thunder rolls, the smirr of rain turning to heavy globs now, splatting hands and backs of necks. Puk up ahead carries Jaq's doublet slung over his shoulder, as Jaq carries Puk's jerkin, sleeves cut off after reckoning Ana's snazzy thus—plus it solved the cuff brevity issue—both playing prudent for the expedition by setting out full-togged, trek boots and everything, both ditching uppers in the mugginess that's built the last hour.

Lookit! says Puk

A dead tree toppled angles from roots still half-rooted down into the gully, spiked with shatterings of branch and wet moss slick on the trunk, it looks an ugly peril, but navigable for the limber—and a canny move to clear the firs towering tight to the gully's edge. So they tightrope it down, arms winged, a skiting foot and jerky flail to rebalance from Puk halfway, Jaq snagging britches on a shard at the last stretch, yanking free, shoogling perilous, springing hard to a muddy splot rather than come a cropper.

The rain is peltering down, wind blattering the trees above, by the time they find an overhang for shelter. Sheet lightning limns the opening heavens, and they count: one element; two elements; three elements; four—the thunder rumbles.

Electric, the skies stance a show for them, fury and sound, only fifteen minutes but *such* a span.

On the way home, cloying damped by the sweat of scrambling boulders and pebbles, and by pissy showers that won't opt to be off or on, they start to drag. Puk groans as another spatter of rain starts up. Jaq cricks his neck and limbers shoulders with a windmill of arms. They rest a stint in a cracking of sunlight that dulls over to move them on, dried just enough to be clammy. At a stretch where the mudbank eats up the pebble edge of the riverbed, Puk slips and planks sideways, right knee and elbow deep into the slop, mudsplat clarting that whole side.

Then: as if to spend all in the final stretch, a shower that starts the same half-arsed patter as every of the last five hundred yonks, cuts loose, and of a sudden it's bucketing again; and Jaq throws his hands out, palms up in luckless trodden supplication—really? *really?*—muttering and flapping ire until he clocks Puk, rivulets running down his face, trying not to smirk.

What?

Puk dints him a link to his own privates, stancings stored for Sifu Renart.

You should see yourself right now.

Jaq calls it up. It's... the pitiful drench of Diogenes in the bath, crossed with a stimhead in full froth.

And it's one of those moments where misery tips into the absurd, the farce of indignity, and suddenly there is no tribulation, just a brace of fleshlings laughing, throwing heads back to strake fingers through their hair as in a scrubber, flinging arms wide to twirl in the deluge, and the folly of hooking arms to birl that lands them both in the mud which tips it all wilder still until, with all the gusto of kidsters jappling in a dub, they're digging hands into the glaur to chuck dods, after which it's pretty much just glorious stupidity.

So, out of the wildwoods they come, finally, droukit and manky, clarty, maukit, traipsing back into more familiar terrain, the carse of the Erehwyreve, fields and foresty steads, and at last crashing through the undergrowth at the bottom of Jaq's sward, the adventurers return triumphant.

•

GROWS ON MOUNTAINS at altitudes between three hundred and seventeen hundred metres, with a rainfall of over a thousand millimetres, reaching forty to fifty metres high, sometimes even sixty, with a trunk diameter of up to five foot, an astringent antiseptic bark, and beneath that bark a timber which is light and soft, durable and pliable, and so was used in the furniture of Pompei and Herculaneum, while the Greeks used his gum, the Menses of Eileithyia, medicinally in childbirth, and the balsam extracted from his harvested oleoresin, Strasburg Turpentine, to preserve new wine, others in other eras using it for perfumes, or for medicine, or for caulking ships, just as they used the residue left from the extraction of Oil of Turpentine as a solvent, rosin oil, for varnishes and lacquers, although here in the scrubber what's in use is actually his flattened needle-like leaves—one point eight to three centimetres long, two millimetres wide, point five millimetres thick, and generally a little notched at the tip, glossy dark green above, with two greenish-white bands of stomata below, and rich with an essential oil, a bronchial sedative, disinfectant, and ingredient of medicine and perfume—which are, like his rheumatics and neuralgia salving rubbing oil resin, as expectorants, common in cold remedies and cough mixtures, whether in lozenge or inhalant, also in folk medicine for bronchitis, cystitis, leucorrhoea, ulcers, flatulent colic, albeit here a simpler use is being made of them in the scented bath products with which the fleshlings cleanse in foamy bubbles and suds, with no small focus on those acute reminders of what he lost in exchange for tall cones, nine to seventeen centimetres long, three to four centimetres broad, with between one hundred and fifty to two hundred scales, each with an exserted bract and two seeds, ripening in the late autumn, disintegrating on maturity to release the winged seeds, that cone which, atop a staff in the thyrsos of Dionysus, was a symbol of the god's phallus, or in the orgiastic rituals of Kybele, high in the mountains, centred on his decorated trunk, of what he snipped off himself on her orders, when she discovered the handsome youth she loved had been unfaithful and transformed him to a large evergreen pyramidal conifer Attis, *Abies alba,* the Silver Fir which

•

WHICH IS WHICH? says the Duke of Burgundy, alighted on the banister of the balcony beyond the french windows, a fat-bodied butterfly who once went by the less grandiose name of Mr Vernon's Small Fritillary, flexing his wings a little, chocolate brown with amber spots.

After the scrub, they lounge on Jaq's fresh-linened bed, a sloth of rampaged Thracian savages with the stead as Persian palace conquered for a pochle of grub and booze, plumbing and cushy nest of duvet and pillows, not to surrender to this decadence of civilisation, honest, just for a wee shift from the puffmat Jaq humphed up to the treehouse—how many weeks ago was that?—just since Renart is in Erehwyna again, visiting Ana, and besides they're knackered, today's jaunt near as trachling as the grand trek of the thunderstorm and Mudfest, as they've come to call it. Not to mention the results of Jaq's experiment in eau d'ardour, cultivating sweat of fuckery in loin and oxter, and a bouquet of mingled jisms liberally spattering tum and chest, mussing pubes, dabbed and swiped with Puk's skivvies, but only so said skivvies could be worn.

Pink evening clouds over darkening blue, outside the sky is fuschia. Getting close to the gloaming enough the Duke of Burgundy might risk being mistaken for a moth, but he did have to flit by and see in full tetrachromatic splendour these fleshlings that are all the buzz, while he still had the stint. He's only got the five days as an adult after all. Five. It's lucky he can't count. While his myriad ommitidia offer from every angle a span of shade beyond the fleshling's violet though—so that sky looks richer yet to the Duke of Burgundy, tasty as a primrose in dappled sunlight—focus is not his forté, so whether it's Puk lolled on the cosy bed and Jak astride him or vice versa is as fuzzy as his piliform-scaled arse.

The plum mumbler is Puk, ouias?

You can't tell? says Susurrus.

Jaq's eyes are acuminate, his jawline acute, his nose gracile. Puk's eyes are ovate-acute, his jawline elliptic, his nose celestial. Jaq's lips are divaricate, Puk's succulent. Jaq's neck is velutionous, his chest... holosericeous but for ciliolate nipples, sauveolent even in the axial flocs, where the scent before the scrub was—seriously, Jaq—distinctly vulpine, verging on hircine. Jaq likes that smell; it's him, both of them. It wasn't *that* bad, was it? Yes, it was. Puk crinkles his neb. Now though... Jaq's abdomen is also holosericerous, becoming lightly pilose in the mesial runnel, in a whorl around umbilical dint, (versus Puk's nubbin,) thickening to hirsute pubic floc.

His pecker is virgate, striving for arborescent under the tongue of a knacky lad.

Thumb sleeking glair over the crinkle of frenulum, down the keel of pintle, brings the tadger full astrut with a jigget. Tongue tip takes over when the grasp reaches root, slicking up the shaft to glabrous seam, then succulent lips and the warm wet plunge beyond that rim, the sucking deep slide of throat set to sheath it all without gag, though, after the wavebeat of unswallowing lunges down and over and drawing back, with a gasp at breaking for air. In a rapture of supplication and mastery, Puk glances Jaq's breathy shock of acute jawline opened wide as a snake's in his gasp, as if at waist-high splash into icewater, and gullets the cock again full, to gaze up now and eyelock, to make eromenos doe-eyes of... not servility exactly but the yen to be subject, in all ways, of his love's regard. An enquiring gaze, asking ardent regard to bask in, silent because it's needless to articulate the question being answered in every gasp and in that wondrous blissom adoration being returned, eye to eye, from Jaq.

He is encompassed himself, in the steering clasp of hand on shoulder and scrubber-fluffed noggin bobbing in prayer to the gods of cock, filled with grace from the sacred font of the phallus.

Then, sensing from quiver of thighs and rising arrhythm of breath and bleat the moment of shift, he bears down to a jiggety blur of hand taking over as he slips back and off mouthwise, so he can watch with bitten lower lip the full glory of the fountain.

A geyser to mock the Pierian Spring, he swanks as Jaq's whoopings and commendations die down. And tasty too.

As if a slice of orange turned out not be there between thumb and forefinger, Puk sooks the crook of his purlicue, smacks lips. He turns the back of his hand up and round, this way and that, to lap up the glop skeeted up to fall, and spurted up to spatter, and squeezed out to spill over it, all the while holding Jaq's eyes with his, all mischief and gloat.

A dip down then, to taste from the spicket with the scrimple of sac below: glans sapid, slightly sweet with fructose, decides the aulete of the tadger astrut. His tongue tip traces and chases, a lapping cat at a spillage. He finishes with a swipe of his palm around Jaq's belly to swab slaver. Whereupon a hand flat on Puk's chest pushes gentle to topple him recumbent, so Jaq can scootch from supine himself, to his knees, then a tappety tug to the Earther's arm to tell him flip, and Puk rolls with a shoogle to prone. Shuffles arse up at the guiding grasp of hips. Feels fingers tease into the groove.

Jaq, of course, as he squeezes the rump afore him and bends to his own task, is already marking the faintest ammonial whiff as a note in his still otherwise pine fresh aroma, and plotting a sneaky play of Puk that will add to it, as he begins again the cultivation of his billy goat's kinabra.

VIII

•

Erehwyna Old Town city-planning of the Neo-Archaic: broad leafy boulevards of Paris; roads lowered to Amsterdam canals in tarmac paralleled by pavements and arced by bridges; off-streets narrowing to London alleys with hints of the Mediterranean or Minoan, fractaling to branched wynds and zigzags, traffic noise rising from the grilled vents of the subroads. A labyrinth, said Puk, as they wove a shortcut from Boulevard Max Keirinckx.

On Hovendaal, Puk looks over balustrade as battlement, in the scent and under the shade of a potted needle cedar, watching the subway scuttle below, pointing out: the quais of Paris with the Seine snipped out, Left Bank and Right stitched together; driveways for dry docks and wharves of garages, arcades of arched doors in bold colours; steps up to the cobbled streets that are rooftops to these townhouse undercrofts. To the right a little ways, a humped bridge crosses from one pavement to the other. To the left, a canopy bridge vaults a crossroads in the spiderweb of reticulated trenches with a cobbled square of gentle camber, kiosk on the near corner where steps serve for the humphing up to it of a delivery from a skimcart parked under.

Tenements of stonework bevelled at the mortared interstices, with lintels over doors and ledges under louvred windows. Lintels are important, according to Sifu Renart, stancing a cue we glean, albeit subwise and seldom noted, but subtly welcoming as a gesture of shelter, to homecomer or visitor. Baroque fuss is for Tempeans, of course, and a clean cut aesthetics of the minimal, the ergonomic, is fit for interior living, even for subrural steads cutting sharp shapes in the forests, but a city must stance itself against any ambience of hive with architectural quirks. A door without a lintel is like a meeting without a kiss hello.

As they turn up an offstreet, Puk's knuckles knock against Jaq's where they stroll side by side, arms brushing as they swing, and he slips his hand round to lace fingers, gets a bump of shoulders, a grin, and a squeeze of the handclasp in return.

It is two weeks, three days, five hours and eight minutes since Jak first clocked Puk on the Left Bank esplanade and... there! That was the thirteenth second, gone in a tick, unlucky for some but a snug click into the Fibonacci Sequence of stints Jaq has just idly noted to this shift.

Above, embroidered tapestries hung from balconies reveal parental pride and kidster fancy in images of feathery dinosaurs, racing gliders, ponies, skimbikes, kittens. Maman Cartier still has Jaq's somewhere in the undercroft, he reveals on prodding, a crude botchwork of sunflowers in a vase which Puk will never see. These add a unity as they cut through the arch of a bastion conversion into the New Town, and the tenements now start to intercut with, until outbred by, Neo-Helladic galeries, in blocks and cram-ins, all cleanlined adobe and skillion roofs, the tapestries hung from oak balconies now. No subroads here, just slim cobbled pavements at undercroft level with stairs to galeries or tenement terraces, then just steps to stilted boardwalks over skimpod buzz, walkways bridging to balconies like twigs off a branch, as with the one they now reach which takes them to the Cartier home.

•

DIOGENES YIVVERY FOR scraps, fidgeting forward in a bum-shuffle and scribble of claw, thudump of hindlegs on parquet flooring that doesn't actually settle him any closer, just advertises his proximity, the cadge. A lick of chops at the taunt of treat forgotten in Jaq's hand, hovering on the verge of offer surely, swayed this way and that to a grousy yowl perfectly translateable as *oh, come on already!* as the blatherskite blabs on.

Jaq the callant is blowsting of grand exploits, conjuring a scene of Don hefting him up with a punty onto Joi's shoulders to grab an edge of wall, scramble up. Down the street, Shim keeks round a corner, keeping edgy, tenty for trouble. Acrobatic at the top, Jaq's picking the apples and tossing them down when—

Jaq! says Maman Cartier. One wastrel in the kin's enough.

Jaq's kidster cousins sit afore him, Verniq and Felis, gawps to his braggadocio, albeit with sporadic shy scrutinies of Puk, who's squeezed in beside Jaq on the sofa, Uncle Bruno on the other side of Jaq talking to Aunt Beatris in her armchair that way, while Puk, in between cardamom and rosewater mouthfuls of Papa Cartier's yazdi cakes, has found himself chitchatting to Aunt Indira, in the arnchair to his side, about... well, this, being plunged into the Erehwynan culture as an outsider, which she knows only too well, coming from Kasei herself. This is not to mention: Robot, lying on Puk's feet; Papa Cartier in constant circuit with his baking; Maman Cartier distributing coffee; Aunt Katje feeding Cousin Hans in the kitchen; Grampapa Cartier and Uncle Jaq out on the balcony, smoking cigars; Cousin Grietje *somewhere around;* and various others whose names and relationships Puk can't remember, all together turning the Cartier abode into a hugger mugger of the extended familial with any hint of spread in the notion of *extended* blithely cannoned to the skies.

It is, for Puk, a keen shift from the previous visits.

First visit, the home was just a strange house with a crazy happy mutt, parentals off visiting and Jaq to tend Diogenes while Puk snuck a chance for a furtive nosey. Second visit was whirlwind, in and out. This time... Jaq's Aunts Beatris and Katje, Maman Cartier's younger sister and her spouse, have just had their second sprog, ickle Hans, so Jaq's namesake uncle, Maman Cartier's brother, is in town with his spouses, Bruno and Indira, and their sprogs, of course, Verniq and Felis, as is Grampapa Cartier, with his mutt, Robot, for the naming feast in Sanderpark tonight, all staying in the Cartier abode, with Katje's parentals here too, and Grampapa and Gramaman Arnaud, Papa Cartier's parentals, dropping by later, and various other kith and kin massing here as jumppoint for the celebrations, or swinging by just to see the sprog and/or family members who haven't been back in Erehwyna for a while. Or maybe just, Puk thinks, to angle for a critical mass of greetings where it takes so long to kiss hello to all another sprog has popped and it's time to start all over again.

Everyone else is at Aunt Elen's, Jaq blithely informed him at one point when he fancied the chaos peaked. You'll meet them all later.

It can be a stagger, ouias? says Aunt Indira. Welcome to Erehwyna!

•

WELCOME TO EREHWYNA. Rumbumtious haggersnash.

Jaq snirtles with a headshake at the tourist in conniption at a skimbooted kidster, bullering at the top of his voice, over a whiz across his path. He apes puffed belligerence, daddles up as if to duke it out, drops it when the tourist glares, but with a shrug and pinky wiggle that stances targeted unrepentance: *ouias, I mean you.*

Argyreans, he says. They come here to quaff till crapulous, bumble through the Old Town nightlife soused, then get all fashing and fratchy that they're *visiting a home with a hound!*

This last, aimed loud at the churl, is local idiom—translated: a good guest shifts to their host's terms, no snits that the family dog isn't kicked outside... or, in this case, that skimboots aren't banned on pavements like back home. Puk can savvy the jostle of near sideswipes from speeding brats, to be fair—it took him months to chill the sense of peril when a flock bursts by you in their flight along the esplanade or whatnot—but he sees the principle. Like Renart says, there is no utopia. Erehwyna wouldn't be Erehwyna without—

Lookit, says Jaq.

He follows the point of Jaq's finger across Market Square. In the road-level plaza lined with awninged undercroft stores, filled on mart days with stalls and booths, buskers and revellers now, he expects some nifty find, sees instead a gathering and parting of crowd at the far corner, Hovendaal and Gunner.

What—?

A flare whooshes wavery into the sky, explodes to a blossom of red stars: a firework.

Out of Hovendaal it comes now, the funeral procession, the quagga-drawn float a small barque of floral wreaths, clear walled furnace atop it, cremation in action, flames fierce around the shrouded form within. Pipes out the top suck smokebelch down into its belly—no chimney, no visible exhaust. And from the base of this, from among the wreaths, fireworks shoot into the night sky, gunshot reports sounding a vermillion peony or scarlet palm, a simple sphere of tailless stars or a thick rising tail of ascent to a burst of comets exploding as fronds. Kamuro and crossette effects are synaesthesia, crimson noise glittering, raucous light crackling.

They're all red, says Puk even as his PAN spills elucidation into nous: red as Helladic symbol of: blood; life; passion; rage. Details of cultural roots on Earth go ignored.

Roman candles mark the pace of the cortège, mourners with crimson satchels and sparklers walking slowstep behind: ffoosh, left; *boom,* left; ffoosh, left; boom, left. It's a strange sight as it does its slow circuit of Market Square—the plaza emptying now as locals and savvy visitors make their way to the edges, dints going out public to the unsavvy, here and there some straggler tourist manhandled to custom by a companion. When all's clear, the float leaves its cortège lining the edges of the square for a slow spiral in toward the centre, where it stops and, as the pyre flames flare and shift in hue to deep rose, limned in blue, the form at the heart of it starts crumbling visibly in the inferno, incinerated before their eyes, fireworks crescendoing in an almighty BOOM, and...

Then... it's over. The flames still burn. Remnants of form remain within them. But the barque moves off, and the mourners break, not to follow but to turn to passers-by, drawing flasks out of their satchels, offering drinks.

Puk watches, unsure of what he's feeling, as Jaq greets an old woman turned to him at random—right hand to hip, left hand to shoulder, kiss on the left cheek, kiss on the right cheek—and takes the offered drink, asks how she knew the dead.

A tap on the shoulder—a middle aged man, a mourner.

Puk steps in to the embrace.

•

KYPARISSOS, CYPRESS, *CUPRESSUS sempervirens*. Son of Telephus, once a lad of Chios, he is a medium-sized evergreen tree growing up to thirty five metres high, often less than a tenth as wide; so: tall and slim as you'd expect of the beloved of Apollo, the eromenos of his erastes, blessed by the god of music, poetry, philosophy, astronomy, mathematics, and science who was once however just a litle mouse god on Tenedos. Blessed by his lover with the customary gift was Kyparissos—a deer, only *his* was tamed.

A tame stag? says Susurrus.

A tame stag, says Kyparissos.

How he loved his pet, his favourite companion, as he loved Apollo and was loved by him, as the two fleshlings walking hand in hand upon the sunlit path, hair tousled by Susurrus, love each other, Puk and Jaq and Jaq and Puk, sard and carnelian, carnelian and sard. The hunting accident, Kyparissos sighs, it broke his heart, the javelin astray, and from his own hands, as his gentle stag lay sleeping in the woods. He's sensitive, he won't deny, sways to the slightest breeze, even the lightest touch from spry Susurrus rippling him all up his height—as now, as the swipper godling of the Martian wind tends him a comforting caress, a hand upon a shoulder stroking down to bicep, or the nuzzle of a faithful pet, a dog or deer, who doesn't savvy your tears but yearns to give you solace. Yes, he's sensitive. A delicate sort, he won't grow back his foliage if pruned too harshly, leading Servius to muse if his association with the underworld was down to this.

What fortitude he lacks though, he makes up for in longevity, with specimens reputed to be over a millennium in age. Why, these here, in the colonnade of slender beauties at the entrance of the Jardins Rochester, for all their limber elegance of stripling pride, have stood for centuries. And he *is* stripling here, in these; elsewhere, elsewhen, he is *immortalised;* look to the plein air paintings of van Gogh, who wrote his brother Theo one July, describing his *canvas of cypresses with some ears of wheat, some poppies, a blue sky like a piece of Scotch plaid; the former painted with a thick impasto like the Monticellis, and the wheat field in the sun, which represents the extreme heat, very thick too.*

This was the gift of his Apollo: wrought by grief, cradling the dying creature in his arms, he begged the god to let his tears fall for eternity; so Apollo turned him to the cypress, with his scale-like leaves, produced on rounded shoots, from two to five millimetres long, this dark green foliage in dense sprays, branchlets variably loosely hanging, as his tears, from the erect or level branches rising, in slim quivers of his sorrow, tremulous, in his fastigiate crown. It's strange, he thinks, how Servius could not see in his longevity and frail grace how he simply *is* memorial; why in Attica, a house in mourning would be garlanded with cypress; why in Rome, statues of Pluto, god of afterlife, of underworld, were decorated with his wreaths; why he was used to fumigate the air during cremations: every cypress is a cenotaph.

Where do the fleshlings go? he asks Susurrus.

Ovoid or oblong, the seed cones that Kyparissos grows are green at first, but after pollination, given something between twenty months and twenty-four, they will mature to brown, reaching a length of twenty-five to forty millimetres, each with ten to fourteen scales, the male cones, three to five millimetres long, releasing pollen in late winter.

The mascherari stall, Susurrus answers.

At the far end of the avenue, it's true, erastes and eromenos now browse the renter's wares: the plain white volto, mannequin blank; the full-face bauta with its snowplow jut of jaw freeing the mouth for hors d'ouvres or aperitifs; the half-face columbina of highwaymen in penny dreadfuls or superhero sidekicks on the silver screens of yesteryear; a black oval moretta with its wide round mirror eyes, all eeriness, inscrutability, strigine and Cycladic; tragedy and comedy, a piange wrung to sorrow's grimace, and a fawkes mask wrinkle-eyed in sly smirk.

It would be, in the Libertine Meadows, bad form to wear more than a sunmask, so the fleshlings strip—plimsolls and plimsolls, Puck's military doublet and Jaq's sleeveless Geister jerkin, Jaq's white britches and Puk's jade and crimson paisley—hand these over to the renter as he raxes them their masks, a columbina each, one sard and one carnelian, each lover in the other's shade of skin.

You know, Susurrus says, as Servius tells it, in some versions of the tale, it's not Apollo you were paired with; it was Zephyros, or Silvanus, spirit of the woods.

A secret for you, Kyparissos whispers in his rustle, if you promise not to tell your father that I told you...

Pinky swear, Susurrus says.

Apollo, Zephyros, Silvanus... I loved them all, they all loved me, and in that aspect they were always, and will always be, one and the same.

•

PASSING THE OLD in one another's arms, birds in the trees, following the tarmac path by the high hedge perimeter, under umbrage of topiary that might have graced Pliny's terrace *adorned with a rendering of diverse animals in boxwood*, they come through an arboreal arch into the Libertine Meadow, green swathe rolling down ahoy them flowered red with poppies and with flesh, kamasutran lotus blossoms of limb-locked lovers here, there, everywhere, a spillage of some erotic cornucopia seeded and sprouting.

Oh, says Puk. Okay.

And yet. He had imagined Romanesque decadence, a bacchanal of anonymous cavorts, piles awhoop and wild wantons bucking in ecstasy, but rather than orgiastic rutting, the air is of leisure. Caligula's wet dreams? Bosch's Garden of Earthly Delights? No, under the glorious sun of Erehwynan summer, in all the fuckery here, there's no transgression to the carnal, no cathartic breach in carnival, no escape; these libertines have long since won the struggle that required defiance of all mores, the stance of combat in their flagrant lusts. Instead, this is Seurat... A Sunday Afternoon on the Island of La Grand Jatte, La Grand Jouissance, La Grand Joie de Vivre.

So:

Puk, even after months of barefoot scrambling, trepid on balls of feet over hot tarmac, cervine in his daintying tread out over the twigs and stones among the shin-high grass, Jaq's seasoned soles allowing steady stride of a hunter, his shaded gaze scanning butterflies and apes, cowgirls and missionaries, crouching tigers and curled angels, they weave a bumblebee's exploration through constellations of couplings—and grouplings, for that matter—the tummocky slope of Libertine Meadow a grassgreen starfield with poppies for its Milky Way and Aretino's postures for its zodiac—designedly, a great circle of sixteen twains having spotsynched to cast the pattern of Raimondi's engravings.

Jaq stakes a patch, dumping the satchel, crouching down to draw the blanket from it, the slickering lotion. Puk sidles up behind to stand, hands resting on Jaq's ferntickled shoulders, feeling... that the park is not Jaq's sward, is not their meadow. But then, maybe they can bring their meadow to the park.

Yesterday:

•

PERFUME AND POISON, worn as a lure to attract mates and as a noxious ward protecting against predators, the sap of *Heliotropium europaeum*, European Heliotrope or European Turnsole, is a slim scent upon the milkweed butterfly which flutters up from one of Klytie's sun-gazing flowers to dance around the sky, perhaps a dozen feet away from where, lazed in the sward that rolls down from the treehouse toward undergrowth and river beyond, Jaq and Puk lie side by side, naked, doing whatever it is they're doing.

Whatever it is they're doing, Klytie doesn't know, doesn't care; Susurrus is whispering his gossip about it to her even now, but she's not really listening and has eyes only for the sun she turns her flowers to, for the godly glory that is Helios, who loved her as a nymph until, as gods are wont to do, he left her for another and, as lovers are wont to do, she wasted quite away and was transformed into her current form.

An annual summer-blooming herb, perhaps because she is so locked in focus on her lost love, blind to what's around her now, Klytie often springs up as a roadside weed. Here, she has found a spot for herself in a quiet meadow any fleshling sun-worshipper would be blithe to lie in and soak up the solar rays, but Klytie would be as happy, like as not, to sprout on the verge of the dustiest, grit-strewn subrural track of Erehwyna, ignoring skimpod's buzz or hiking gaggles of tourists atromp with dropped cigar butts and piss-streams into bushes—just as long as they don't dawdle to gawp gormless and block her sun, as Alexander seeking wisdom of Diogenes. Growing from a taproot to reach maximum heights near forty centimeters, her stem is covered in soft hairs, as too her oval leaves, as too the fuzzy, bristly sepals of her inflorescences, coiled spikes of white flowers, each bloom a mere few millimeters wide.

A bumpy nutlet, her fruit. A nutty bumplet, her nous, such that it is, as far as Susurrus is concerned. To call it a one track mind might be inaccurate, imply dimensional extension in what's more a dot, a focus tightened to the keen intensity of her beloved's rays through a lens in the hand of a firestarting kidster. There's no getting through to her, really. Still, she is pretty, and Susurrus can't help but idly flirt with her, as with every flower and blade of grass.

They're singing now, he says. Listen, it's sweet. And it's about the sun, right up your street.

That perks her interest a little, and though she keeps her gaze as always locked upon the sun, she lets the sound slip into her nous now. Susurrus isn't lying either; it is sweet, some modern translation of a hymn as old as civilisation itself, to Aton-Ra, to Helios in a fiercer face. She lets the melody serve as articulation of her own adoration, stancing keen in her sway to Susurrus's touch, out of time but aptly so, the strain of unsynching spot on for her yen, as if to plead: See? See? They speak for me.

Fleshlings are good for that, at least, for singing to her beloved for her. Some ring of chanting men on a summer morn, she thinks, singing *their boisterous devotion to the sun*—as some ancient poet once scribed it, like as he too had a Jardins Rochester orgy in his line of sight, as Klytie has on many an occasion, from another vantage. Yes, let the fleshlings sing, and let their song carry her love to Helios, and let him return it that she may bask.

The vacuum of space is silent, you know, Susurrus reminds her, no air to carry the sound.

Oh, but she can imagine the roar of the sun, if one could stand in its corona, photons torrenting into your eyes or petals, into every fibre of you.

Today:

•

Puk on his back, legs astraddle and akimbo as in a mid-air crouch, left hand of Jaq's on the ball of Puk's right heel, pushing back, Jaq's cock to the root, pubic brush pressing in to the valleying curve of buttocks in to splendid socket, tupping that splendid rump from Canova's Perseus or Corrigan's porn.

All rituals duly followed, all gifts given, scenes enacted, the harpagmos is complete, but they remain, and will remain, erastes and eromenos. For all that the cycles of such summer schooling should, in theory, call for a graduated Puk to step on in the togs of older lad and find his own eromenos, for all that this archaic snoot or that might cock to a man being unmanned by piercing fuckery, as passive kinaidos, Alexander and Hephaestion were agelings. So they'll fuck forever, both have sworn, in Erehwyna that's as much a country for old men and women, says Renart, as much as anyone.

They shrugged it off, the Greeks, yesterday's eromenos become today's kinaidos. You can lift up a bull, they said, if you carried the calf.

•

Landscape is language in the Jardins Rochester, formal geometry toppled into a tumble of more dynamic articulation, ordered by grammar as Capability Brown would have it, in his explanation to Hannah More.

Now *there*, said Brown, I make a comma, and there where a more decided turn is proper, I make a colon; at another part, where an interruption is desirable to break the view, a parenthesis; now a full stop, and then I begin another subject.

Tomorrow:

•

EARL GREY, SAYS Puk, Maine Coon, waltz, sea salt, pink champagne, apple, reason.

Espresso, says Jaq, Irish Wolfhound, polka, black pepper, ruby port, cheese, passion, bedsuite.

Earl Grey, says Puk, Maine Coon, waltz, sea salt, pink champagne, apple, reason, kitchen.

In the game of Fourier Harmonies, Puk has it easy, cued by Jaq's extension to find his own in the complement, and Jaq has conceded, in the interests of indolence, that binaries are allowed. So, he lazes with Jaq as pillow, gazes the wee black bumclock crawling along the forefinger held above him, iridescent blue-black little dor beetle like a miniature scarab. He lolls, riposting with reflex flips, enjoying the game more for the fremitus of Jaq's voice felt ear to chest than for the sport.

Espresso, says Jaq, Irish Wolfhound, polka, black pepper, ruby port, cheese, passion, bedsuite, *sex*.

•

A BRIGHT RED spring and summer flowering perennial, as *Papaver somniferum* here, as *Papaver rhoeus* there, Mêkôn grew naturally amongst the wheat fields of the ancients, long before they thought to plant him, in their crop rotations, to revitalise the soil. Pure and simple in his brilliance of four petals, cleancut as a carved design of quatrefoil symmetry, perfection in a posey, he might seem the apotheosis of his cultivation, the most manicured artifice of a scarlet blossom, but he has always been and will remain a wildflower at heart.

When his poppy seeds were not being used in cakes baked for the mysteries of Demeter, as his bold blooms themselves adorned festivities, they were instead, as he recalls with no small joy, being turned to other relishable pursuits, strong opiates extracted from them for the wilder celebrants in those same cults. From the poppy juice dripping from the wand of Hypnos, god of sleep, to the squirt of heroin from a syringe, he has always offered dissolution of raw pain to oceanic pleasure, bliss so far beyond restraint and reason many fleshlings lost themselves within his raptures. He makes no apologies for his addictive charms, his outright seductive snaring of dreamers decadent or desperate, seeking inspiration or escape. He is relief. He is release. And if wars have been fought over his trade, empires established in gunship or garotte, he has been medicine too, he has been mercy.

A youth beloved of the goddess Demeter, upon his early death in some tragedy long since forgotten in his heady haze, he was transformed by her into a poppy flower, and was so touched by her kind spirit of remembrance that he never once forgot it, never once forgot—though all else slipped from his mind—her generosity of metamorphosis, so that even centuries, millenia on, when she herself was long since gone, untempled and unmysteried, a hollow lesson of Greek lore and Latin echoes to be learned by schoolboys in starched collars, he himself sought to reiterate her mercy for those boys in a foreign land far from the classrooms of their youth.

He remembers how he swathed himself over the silenced fields, to cloak the gun-churned mire of blood and the buried, first in the pointillism of green grassy shoots dotting sparse the sombre dark brown ground, then in the thickened lightened verdancy as a tipping point was turned so the surface sang in a bright fuzz of Spring; and finally, when the Somme was meadow, he opened his red bloom of sixty thousand remembrances to the sun. Sixty thousand in one day, and more, and he carries all of them in him now, obliviated and preserved.

•

AND IN THE meadow, pillowed by Jaq's chest, Puk tells of how his apostate Da and Mam were scythed in an epiphany bombing one day while in the city, some teenage zealot—teenage in Earther years, he checks—eyes afire with oaths of apotheosis for all, expediting the raptures of all, crying *liberation from the flesh* as he stood for the sniper to detonate a sunlight lobotomy in his frontal lobe, the dead man's switch slipping from his grip as he crumpled, and there was a flash as bright as the boy must've seen, and it brought the building down, the whole building down on top of everyone, and then it was all over.

Except it wasn't, it wasn't over, as for all his father's disavowals of geisting, his own geisted kin petitioned kith, his own father and grandfather and great-grandfather and so on back to pilgrim forefather Brigham Massinger who was of the first returnees scrabbling the barren soil now hight the Heartland, and of the first raptured to virtual paradise as reward; they set to swaying the Ancestry over the prodigal, and doctors' decrees wormed the will to naught, arguing immorality, insanity, illegitimacy, no right to abort eternity; so they had to attend, Puk and Ana, had to attend the wake of their parents' geists, say adieu to the flesh and bienvenue to the shade of psyche. Vanguard of the queued celebrants, front of line for the alohas. Shimmering geists of their ancestors filling the backhall beyond the podium where Da and Mam Massinger glimmered into afterlife. Blinked down at daughter and son.

Ana squeezed his hand so tight then, to soothe which one of them he didn't know, in her need or in savvy of his. He squeezed back just as tight, tighter maybe, feeling helpless bothways, in his need and in savvy of hers.

Worst of it is, Puk tells him in thicket voice, how he ached to believe it. The essence of them uploaded from the implants, living on, saved.

His Mam's geist it was though, true to that essence, told them straight it wasn't them. Said it just as eggshell gentle as she would have, on her knees to cradle his teary face; but that's the thing about a perfect sim of a psyche: why would it lie if it was aping the savvy it'd be deceit, the burden of empathy?

After.

After, there was the fight for his custody, him not twenty-one yet and the doctors set to huchle him off to a sodality, his sis a spitting fury in defiance.

It shouldn't matter because it's not them, he says, and Ana says they're not even really aware, no more than a sim of your stancing, innards and all.

Yanked, whispers Jaq then: sorry, that's just... yanked is stunted, saying it's stunted is stunted, I don't know what to say it's so...

Rotted, says Puk.

•

KALAMOS, *ACORUS CALAMUS*, even his name seems calmly sonorous to Susurrus, fit to the hushing soughs they make in smoothing one through the other, wind and reed caressing soft as skin ever felt on skin. He is a tall perennial wetland monocot with scented leaves of edges wavy like a fluttering pennant, from which he gains the nickname Sweet Flag, and with rhizomes of an even stronger scent thought to be a powerful aphrodisiac in antiquity, in the Orient and Egypt. Susurrus does not doubt it.

Thought to be psychoactive too he was, now and then, though this lore may be less than reliable. What is sure: this son of the Karian river Maiandros has been a strewing herb, and the source of fragrances, has been used medicinally and as a stimulant, among the northern Native Americans; in Greece and through Europe, from the days of Dionysus, his rhizome was often added to wine, while absinthe found one of its possible ingredients in the root itself; his leaves, with their curly-edged or undulate margins, are between point seven and one point seven centimetres wide, averaging one centimetre over all, the sympodial leaf somewhat shorter than the vegetative leaves; and the spadix, at the time of expansion, may reach a length between four point nine and eight point nine centimetres. Longer than *Acorus americanus*, as are the flowers, at between three and four millimetres.

Little wonder then that his seed spikes on their tall stalks were a phallic symbol—with a wry comment perhaps, on nature's part, in the shriveled look of the abortive ovary he shows, infertile.

Infertile in that respect, anyway. Kalamos has been lush through the ages: in the ink verse born from a reed pen, the qalam of Arabic calligraphy; in the music conjured from his hollow stalks by Pan, on the banks of the river Ladon, birthing the nymph Syrinx in his song, to be loved and chased by the horned god, ever in flight as song must ever be; in the inspiration of Whitman's "Calamus," surely the grass, the leaves, at the heart of his Leaves of Grass, this reed sprung from the lad who lost his lover Karpos in a swimming contest, who chose to let himself drown too rather than live without his eromenos.

Karpos was your half-brother, Ares has told Susurrus sadly, your father's son. Inherited that bright-eyed mischief Zephyros still beguiles with, when he's of a mood for devilry. Not unlike one little imp we might mention, eh, monkey?

You remind me of him, Kalamos has told Susurrus—smiling while he said it though.

So, the Martian godling of the wind, incorrigable flirt Susurrus, slides himself through the tall grass of Kalamus, in this warm summer tomorrow on the banks of a small tributory of the Rio Erehwyreve, where Jaq and Puk swing from a hemp rope to crash wildly in the water, their carouse of shouting nekkid joy unbound so all that's drowned here is the gentler fuckery of the warm breeze and the reeds forming a single voice that whispers Whitman, drowned out as the lovers, Puk and Jaq, cavort, as these two boys together, clinging in the babble of river, each the other loving, splashing, never leaving, swim.

Are you prepared to enter acclaimed author Hal Duncan's world of scruffians and scamps and sodomites? Beware, for it is filled with the gay pirate gods of Love and Death, immortal scoundrels, and young men who find themselves forced to become villains. But who amongst us does not adore a gamin antihero? These fantastical tales from the fringes of an imaginative realm of supernatural fairies and human fey will captivate the reader. Light a smoke, raise a cup of whiskey, and seek a careful spot to cruise the Scruffians!

A finalist for the British Fantasy Awards 2015 for Best Collection!

Acclaimed author and critic Hal Duncan turns his analytic eye towards the development and current state of speculative fiction in the pages of Rhapsody. Duncan's trademark wry humor and suffer-no-fools approach to critiquing the genre will make this book more than a resource for students of the field—anyone who enjoys reading tales of the fantastical and strange can find Duncan's insight worthwhile to read again and again.

ABOUT HAL DUNCAN

Hal Duncan is the author of VELLUM and INK, more recently TESTAMENT, and numerous short stories, poems, essays, even some musicals. Homophobic hatemail once dubbed him "THE.... Sodomite Hal Duncan!!" (sic), and you can find him online at www.halduncan.com or at his Patreon for readings, revelling in that role.

www.ingramcontent.com/pod-product-compliance
Ingram Content Group UK Ltd.
Pitfield, Milton Keynes, MK11 3LW, UK
UKHW040010200726
13854UKWH00001B/121